CW01587624

Praise for

"An excelle _____ stories of the supernatural. People like M.R. James and Arthur Machen. Heady company to be in!" **Stephen King**

"A profoundly moving and genuinely eerie tale about the cruel, persistent horrors of this world, about roads not taken, about love and grief, about courage and sacrifice, about what we do with the time we are given...an extraordinary, utterly unforgettable debut. A beautiful ode to goodness." **Rachel Harrison, USA Today bestselling author of *So Thirsty* and *Black Sheep***

"Somewhere between the cosmic precision of John Langan, the undulating mundanity of Robert Aickman, and the boundless heart of Stephen King, sits Neil McRobert's *Good Boy*. This is an expertly executed story." **Nat Cassidy, USA Today bestselling author of *When the Wolf Comes Home* and *Mary***

"Assured, heartfelt horror firmly rooted in affection, longing and loss and a quiet Northern resignation to things beyond any earthly control. This is a haunting little sting of a book, a sharp nip at the heels." **Gemma Amor, Bram Stoker and British Fantasy Award nominated author of *Itch***

"There's good dogs, there's excellent writers, and there's extraordinary novellas. What you're holding in your hands now is all three." **Stephen Graham Jones, author of *The Buffalo Hunter Hunter***

"*Good Boy* is a magical thing, a story where a grander battle of evil versus innocence is made intimate, personal, small enough to hold in your hand ... I read this in one sitting. I fucking loved it." **Chuck Wendig, author of *The Staircase in the Woods***

"A chilling tale that breaks your heart ... written with the elegiac flood of Dylan Thomas and the homespun verve of a fireside ghost story told at the local pub." **Clay McLeod Chapman, author of *Wake Up and Open Your Eyes***

"The brilliance of *Good Boy* lies in what is suggested: an ageless battle between good and evil, happening in a place we cannot fathom, only the tip of which we see, in the form of a thin man in grey and a small but mighty dog. Just extraordinary." **Josh Malerman, New York Times bestselling author of *Bird Box* and *Incidents Around the House***

"Both terrifying and deeply heartfelt. Echoing the best of Stephen King, it's a story of monstrous horror and quiet sacrifice ... I loved this very English monster story, and I especially loved the titular good boy. You will, too." **Trevor Henderson, author of *Scarewaves***

Good Boy

Neil McRobert

Wild Hunt Books

Good Boy
First published in 2025 by Wild Hunt Books
wildhuntbooks.co.uk

Copyright © 2025 by Neil McRobert
Neil McRobert asserts the moral right to be identified as the author of this
work.

This novel is entirely a work of fiction. The names, characters and incidents portrayed in it are the work of the author's imagination. Any re-
semblances to actual persons, living or dead, events or localities are entirely
coincidental.

A CIP catalogue record for this title is available from the British Library

Paperback: 978-1-0685631-0-2
Ebook: 978-1-0685631-1-9

Cover Design by Luísa Dias
Edited by Ariell Cacciola
Typeset by Wild Hunt Books

The Northern Weird Project is a registered trademark of Wild Hunt Books

*For G, who gave me a home that
I'm always happy to be in.*

*And for Ted, who gives me a reason
to leave it every single day.*

Meetings

FOUR DAYS AFTER LITTLE Andy Hoyle disappeared, Margie Jones caught a man digging in the field where the boy was last seen.

Locals called it the Square, always had, though looking through her kitchen window as her soup simmered on the stovetop, Margie thought the plot's weird angles hardly supported its name. It was an untidy grass field boxed in by ancient drystone walls, a long sweep of Sheephead Lane, and Margie's garden fence. At the top, near the lane, the ground was flat and empty save for a rusted set of swings that creaked in the wind. From there the Square sloped gently downhill to a tangle of longer grass that gathered rainfall like a sponge and threatened to flood her yard every summer. She'd complained over the years but had never been able to ascertain who the land ultimately belonged to, or what its original purpose had been. It was a windy mile of walking to get up here from Symester, and in nearly twenty years living beside the Square, Margie had never seen it put to any use beyond dog walking or children's games.

Don used to complain about the noise the kids made, but she always shushed him. They had to play somewhere, didn't they? And with the town's park full of needles, dogshit and dirty old men – if the letters pages of the *Symester Free Press* were to be believed – where were they supposed to go? At least the Square was safe.

Well, she'd been proven wrong on that front.

For the hundredth time since Andy vanished, she wondered if she might have seen or heard anything that could help the police and the boy's desperate mother. Margie's was one of four terraced houses running close alongside the Square, but neither she nor her neighbours had noticed anything out of the ordinary.

That Sunday afternoon she'd been vaguely aware of the usual chuckle of children's voices, a memory confirmed by Andy's friends, who told the police how they had left him there, just after four, because they had to get home to their tea. Andy had wanted to carry on playing, they said, and with the naivety of village children, they left him doing kick-ups near the apple tree. That's where the police found his ball the next morning, despite his mother's certainty that her football-obsessed son would never willingly leave it behind.

Margie's attention kept wandering to that tree. It stood alone in the southwest corner, on the edge of the long grass, at the furthest point from the houses and the road.

Furthest from safety.

What had it witnessed, she wondered? If the police could quiz the starlings on what they had seen from its branches, what songs would they sing?

The tree's limbs were empty now, as evening fell.

Margie's breath caught in her throat.

There was a man in the shadow of the bough. He was digging a hole.

Even through the distortion of old glass and low winter light, she couldn't fail to recognise him. He was part of her ecosystem, as much as the thrushes that woke her in the morning and the bats that flitted around her gutters on August nights. She didn't know his name, but she'd waved to him over the garden fence a thousand times – him and his little dog on their daily walks.

There was no dog now. Just this man and his shovel. Only days after a child was taken.

Taken.

It was a nasty word, hard in the mouth and in the heart. No one official had yet said it aloud, but Margie had a sinking feeling that people in Symester would be hearing it soon.

She scanned the road. There were no signs of the vehicles that had choked the lane in recent days. No reporters, no ghoulish sightseers up from the village, nor the well-meaning with their flowers and teddy bears. Not a single police car. Without any forensics, or even footprints to go on, the police had moved their enquiries elsewhere — there was rumour of an uncle with a dodgy past — but surely they must still be keeping an eye on the area?

Maybe she should phone the police? That's what Don would have done, but Don was always a cautious man. It was perhaps that overabundance of caution that stopped his heart and left her a widow at fifty-eight. Margie didn't go in for that kind of worrying. Forty years working on the frontline of psychiatric care had mostly cauterised her nerve endings.

Oh, but she had common sense. Plenty of that, and as she slipped into her wellies by the kitchen door, it spoke up in her dead husband's voice.

What are you doing, Margie? He could be dangerous.

Don's anxiety pursued her all the way to her garden gate.

Ducking under the police tape, she nearly went arse-over-teapot on the wet ground. After nights of rain the Square was so boggy that a policeman she'd previously fed and watered had complained that whatever evidence there may have been was well washed away by now.

Soft ground must help with the digging though.

The man worked his shovel with a grinding rhythm. Down, twist, lift, twist, repeat. Despite the late October chill, he'd shucked his jacket, and as Margie approached, she saw his bony frame push against the back of his shirt. He wasn't young: somewhere in the deep end of his sixties, like her, maybe a little older. His collar-length wave of silver hair was full and lustrous, too thick for the wrinkled apple head that it grew from.

Behind him, sitting on a knuckle of exposed tree roots, there was a leather holdall.

Is the boy in there?

Of course not, Don. It's far too small.

Not if he chopped him up.

Don't be absurd, Margie admonished. If this man was burying a body he'd be a bit more bloody alert, wouldn't he? And why would he come back here in the first place?

Don fell silent.

Still, Margie felt vulnerable. The light was leaving at pace, as it always did at this time of year, when the hilltops became teeth and chewed down the sun for an afternoon snack. There was no one else around, not a single car had passed up or down the lane, nor did she expect one. Sheephead Lane was little travelled since the bypass had been put in between Symester and Crowther. That quietude was one of the reasons that she hadn't moved in the years since Don's passing. Margie knew she could have made a nice bit from selling up and buying somewhere smaller in the village, but there were too many people down there, too much traffic and coffee shop gossip. Up here it was just her, a few neighbours, and the quiet. If sometimes she got lonely, if now and then she missed Don with an acid burn that felt like it could melt the gears of her heart, well, the village babble wouldn't cure that anyway.

The man was less than thirty feet away. She could hear the squelch of mud beneath her boots, but he remained oblivious to her approach.

He paused and arched his back. Margie winced at the sound of vertebrae clicking into place.

"Er, excuse me," she said, only strides away.

"Bloody hell!"

The man took a startled sidestep and caught his foot on the shovel head. As he fell, the crack in his knee was twice as loud as the crinkle of his spine.

"Oh, you bastard. You bloody bastard thing."

He rolled on the ground, both hands clasped to his knee, eyes screwed shut.

Margie rushed over. Once a nurse always a nurse. It left you unable to ignore someone's pain, even if they might be a murderer.

"Oh, Christ," he groaned.

"Let me look at it."

Margie prised his hands away. Even through the heavy trousers, she could already feel the swelling joint. "I think it might be dislocated."

"No, it's not," he gasped. "It pops out and it pops back in again. It's happened all my life. Hurts like fu…" He looked at her sheepishly. "Hurts a lot."

"Don't worry," she said. "I've heard worse. You need to go to hospital."

He shook his head and struggled to a sitting position.

"Give me a minute and I'll be right. I'll limp for a week, but I'll live."

"What about walking your dog?"

She meant it as a joke, slightly more confident that he wasn't up to anything sinister, at least not anything involving Andy Hoyle. A man who didn't want to say fuck in front a woman his own age was unlikely to be capable of hurting a child. But a new flavour of pain creased his face at her question, and a thought occurred to her.

Margie looked at the hole. It was no more than three feet across.

She looked at the holdall. Far too small for a human body.

She looked at the man. His jaw still churned with pain, but his eyes were red and swollen. He looked like he'd been crying.

"What's your name?" she asked.

"James. Jim. Jim Howarth."

"I'm Margie Jones."

"Pleased to meet you," he said through gritted teeth. "All things considered."

"What are you burying, Jim?"

He dropped his eyes.

"Jim?"

"I'm sorry. I need to bury him here," he whispered like a chastened child.

"Who, Jim?" She thought she knew the answer.

"Riot."

Margie felt her tension loosen a notch.

"Is he... is he in the bag?"

Jim nodded.

He didn't look guilty at all, only upset and a little embarrassed. But Margie had to be sure. She could all too easily imagine the questions when the police and reporters came streaming to her door.

You didn't check?

You just let this bloke just go?

"Can you show me, Jim?"

"Why?" He looked confused. Then his eyes widened. 'Oh god, you think ...Oh god!'

"Just show me, Jim. I'm sorry."

Jim deflated.

"Aye, help me up."

She took hold of a forearm rigid with muscle. He was old but still strong, and if his fangs were going to come out, it would be now.

But he just huffed to his feet and shuffled to the bag. He looked down at it with sorrow.

"I'm sorry. I... I can't."

She remembered her own shocked, scoured reflection on the night that Don died. If it was possible, Jim's grief looked harsher still.

Slowly, still ready to run at the first threatening move, Margie unzipped the bag. It parted into a tear-shaped pool of darkness, much deeper than the shadows that had fallen around them.

A smell wafted out.

Death. That smells like death.

But the meaty hint of mortality was undercut by a surprisingly sweeter scent.

"Is that coconut?" she asked.

"It's the shampoo."

"Shampoo?"

"I washed him after he died," Jim spoke softly. "It seemed right."

Margie took out her phone and turned on the torch. She pointed it down at the bag to reveal a small shape that she half-recognised, a bundle of golden fur nestled in a faded shirt.

"Riot?" she asked.

"Aye."

"I'm so sorry."

Jim took a shaky breath.

"When did he die?"

"Five nights past."

No wonder the perfume couldn't fully mask the funk emanating from the bag. Even in these colder days, that was a long time for anything to go unburied. Didn't vets have a method for disposing of dead pets?

That wasn't the important question though, was it?

"Why are you burying him here, Jim? Especially now, with all what's gone on?"

"You won't believe me," he said. "You'll think I'm mad."

"Look." Margie could still find a note of charge-nurse severity when the need arose. "I've come out here in my bloody wellies thinking you're a murderer, only to find you messing up a crime scene to bury your dog. I don't know how much madder you think this could look."

"I thought if I buried him here it might save the next one."

"Next one?"

"The next kid."

Margie's head was spinning.

"What next child? Save them from what?"

"From the monster." Jim looked like the wanted to gulp the word back down his throat the moment he said it.

In the long silence that followed, Margie heard the pop of her own joints as she unbent. Jim coughed. He couldn't meet her eyes.

He's a madman, love.

A crackpot.

Get back inside and lock the door.

It turned out her husband was far harder to shush in death than he had ever been in life.

Jim leaned heavily on his good leg; the shovel tucked under his arm in a makeshift crutch. Maybe it was an act, but Margie had patched up enough walking wounded and weekend warriors over the years to recognise a man in genuine pain.

Margie love, don't you dare—

She snipped Don's voice off cleanly. Certainly, Jim didn't sound well. Talk of monsters wasn't a sign of solid mental health, but he didn't scare her. Decades of working with the mentally ill gave you a sense of the potential danger inside a person. But Margie had found the vast majority of unwell people to be frightened rather than frightening. Most were exhausted by their own fear, and Jim looked tired to his marrow.

A car swept along the Lane and she wondered if the headlights had caught their bizarre tableau. Was the driver calling the police right now to report two strange people loitering where that poor boy went missing? Time would tell.

For now, there was just the two of them, a hole, and a dead dog.

"Jim," she said. "Do you want a cup of tea?"

This is mad, love.

Margie let the bubbling kettle drown out her dead husband's angst. She agreed. It was a bad horror movie mistake; the kind that had audiences groaning.

"I might as well be running upstairs in my negligée, eh, Jim?"

"What?" he startled.

"Like in the films. When some soppy young girl runs upstairs rather than out the door, away from the bloke with an axe. Not that you have an axe. And not that I'm a girl." She gestured to herself. "No one wants to look at this in a see-through nightie, do they?"

Jim reddened.

The kettle reached its crescendo and clicked off. Margie turned back to it with relief. She was no good with strangers. Never had been. It wasn't that she said the first thing that came into her head, more like the third of fourth thing, with no chance of the other person understanding how she'd got there. The poor bloke probably thought she was propositioning him, and she'd never seen a man who looked less open to an impromptu tussle.

Jim sagged in the dining chair, his injured leg stretched out on the pouffe she'd brought through from the front room. Margie didn't want to take him any further than the kitchen. She hadn't had a strange man in her home who wasn't here to fix something or check the meter since Don died. She wasn't daft; the kitchen would do fine, thank you very much. In here she had quick access to the back door.

Margie plonked his tea on the table and took her own seat.

"You had that dog a long time, didn't you?

"Longer than most."

"I've lived here seventeen years, and I don't think there's a day gone by that I haven't seen you walking him round out there. He must have been some age?"

"Aye, he was an old boy at the end."

"You must miss him very much."

Jim said nothing. Margie supposed no reply was necessary. Share your life with anything for long enough and it becomes a part of you. Margie thought that went double for husbands and dogs. In her experience, both loved you well beyond the limits of reason, and when that love went away, it was a ship sinking, dragging everything else down.

Jim certainly loved Riot. So much that he'd refused to leave him outside. When she'd balked at him bringing the bag indoors, he'd turned around as if to limp back to his burial. Margie wasn't one for backing down, but she also had a problem with curiosity. Talk of monsters and an answer to where Andy Hoyle might be: they were reason enough to let him bring his dog inside.

So, Riot lay by the back door, safe in his brown leather casket.

"What's this about a monster, Jim? Do you know who took that boy?"

He sipped his tea. Margie watched the cup tremble all the way to his lips, but not a drop spilled.

"It's not a who," he said.

"I'm sorry?"

"It's not a person. Maybe it was once. I don't know. But not for a long time."

"Oh, come off it. You're not telling me there's an *actual* monster knocking around."

"You asked."

She was getting exasperated again. "There's a child missing and his mother's losing her mind. The last thing we need is you telling fairy tales."

He slammed a palm down on the table. Margie jumped back in her seat.

"Now just you wait a bloody minute—" she started.

Here we go, Don said, sounding almost smug.

"Look," Jim said.

Margie stared. Jim's wrist was the rose-pink of healthy flesh, but from the base of his thumb to the tips of his fingers, the hand looked like ancient meat. His entire palm was a crazed cartography of whorls and wrinkles.

"Is that a fairy story?" he challenged.

"What happened to your hand?"

"That's the part that went inside," he said. "And now that poor boy. I hate to think of it."

He shuddered.

"Inside?"

Get him out of here, love. Now.

Margie felt off-balance. Maybe Don was right, but she was just so intrigued. If this was a delusion, it was an interesting one at least.

For the first time Jim held her gaze. He had nice eyes, she noticed. A boy's bright eyes in an old man's haunted face.

"Tell me what you know, Jim."

And he did.

Tellings

It was a Sunday in early 1961. I know that much, because I'd just turned eleven. Maybe it was late January, maybe the very start of February. It's funny how things like that get muddled. I can remember almost every second of what happened that day but not what month it was.

To be fair, you shouldn't have life-changing days at that age. They're supposed to come later, when you can recognise them: falling in love, getting married, children, all of that. When I was eleven the most important things in life were football, horror films, and Katherine Corder. The first I did with my mates. The films were for my dad and me. Katherine was a secret I kept just for myself.

Aye, I suppose the falling in love part doesn't always wait until you're grown. There's no memory from a time before I worshipped Katherine Corder. We grew up a street apart; me on Darwin Street, her on Whittaker Drive, and my dad said we played together when we were really little. But she was two years older than me, and by the time we were both in big school, that gap was as wide as the English Channel.

She's the reason I was in the Square so late that afternoon. Usually, I'd have been home watching *Danger Man* or *Target Luna,* but Katherine was still there, on the swings with Diane Price and Emily Lumb. It's mad how those names come back to you after sixty years. Though I suppose I've good reason to remember poor Emily's name, what with everything that happened.

All three were lovely looking girls. You couldn't have pulled us lads away with packhorses. They were watching us play football and we threw ourselves around energetically, playing dirty and trying to look tough while they swung and giggled. But they weren't mean. Katherine never was. She was kind in that complacent way that pretty girls can afford to be. Girls like her, they toss smiles like princesses throwing favours, not knowing what it means to us fighting for them in the crowd. They cheered every time one of us scored a goal, but when I managed a particularly good save, Katherine singled me out with a "well done, James".

Cue a lot of hooting from my mates.

"Well done, *Jaaames*," Gordon Fox said, like he'd never heard my name before. That set Diane off cackling.

"Ignore them, James," Katherine said.

"He's called Jim," Gordon shouted.

"Well, I know him as James. I don't know *your* name at all."

Gordon sneered, but I could tell she'd winded him. I tried to give a Katherine a smile that conveyed my gratitude, my respect, and all my unceasing devotion, but I probably just looked simple.

"Come on," Emily said, smirking. "If I don't get home soon, my mam will tan my backside." She pointed at me and continued, "Careful that one doesn't follow you home, Kath. He's smitten."

I blushed up to my temples. Hot blood pushing up against cold air.

The minute the girls left, us lads lost interest in the game. We'd been freezing for the last half hour, but no one wanted to be the first to give in. With my jacket thrown down as a goalpost, I'd turned half-blue. Disappointed as I was to see Katherine leave, I was ready to get home. It's more than a mile from the Square down to our end of town, and the afternoon was only getting colder.

I shouted for Herbie Booth to pass me the ball. It was mine and a good one, too. A brand new leather Casey, as we used to call them. Herbie sent it skimming across the grass, but Gordon intercepted it. He chipped it up into the air and, before I could object, he booted it. The ball sailed high and wide, right down the Square and into the long grass by the bottom wall.

"Ooops." Gordon laughed.

"Go and get it," I ordered.

"Your ball, your fetchies." He was already joining the other lads on their way to the gate.

He'd done it on purpose. Gordon always had that nasty steel in him, and either me getting Katherine's attention, or her putting him down had exposed its shine. He was one of my best mates, but did I even like Gordon Fox? Maybe not. Liking someone never seemed to matter that much back then. You were mates or you weren't. It had more to do with proximity and shared enemies than anything else.

"At least, wait for me!" I called.

Herbie Booth looked back, but Gordon grabbed him in a headlock and dragged him towards the gate.

I grumbled down to the long grass. Whoever owns the Square, they had never cut it, so it was a winter corpse, brittle and slimed. Shadows pooled between hummocks of rotten leaves and it took me several minutes of kicking through the mulch before I found the ball. I was cautious 'cos just the week before some of the older lads had found a dead dog half-buried in the grass. Whoever was in charge of such things would've moved it by then, but I hated the thought of my foot striking the cold meat of its body. I must've disturbed something's rest because I heard the scratch and scurry of a small body fleeing my path.

By the time I emerged, my trousers were soaked past the knee and the lads were long gone. That probably sounds bad to you, that they left me, but we were boys; we only felt so much responsibility for each other. If some other kids had stormed the Square that day to pick a fight, as they sometimes did, we'd have stood up for each other without question. But walking a mile home, that they were happy to let me do alone.

Have you noticed that there's a quiet that falls over that field sometimes? That afternoon, it came down like a shutter on a shop window. The light had purpled and I could feel the threat of snow. It was definitely time to get home.

Halfway to the gate, that's when I saw him.

Him? Is that anywhere close to the right word?

The gate closed with a creak when he came through it and he was already inside when I looked up. We both stopped a few yards from each other, cowboys about to go for our guns.

He looked like my grandad.

I don't mean to say he resembled him. Not at all. He had a thin face, far too narrow for the smile that cracked it open. His teeth were tiger bright, and there were a lot of them. Big, chunky teeth. American teeth, my mam would've said. Inside his clothes, he was all angles. He was spindly, like he'd struggle in a stiff breeze. Nothing like the bullish bulk of my grandad.

It was the clothes. He wore the same colourless overalls as my grandad, under the same kind of thick corduroy jacket. A quarryman's outfit, if ever I saw one. His flat cap was *just* like the one grandad wore every day. The old fella always used to tap the reinforced felt and ask me what good would that do if a boulder fell on his head? "Such is the quarryman's gamble," he'd say.

In the end it wasn't the stone that killed him; it was the drink. He'd died the year before and our house was still full of my mam's sadness.

For a half-second I thought maybe this was the old fella come back to visit. I don't remember being scared by the notion, but maybe that's hindsight. Maybe, I simply know now how much better his ghost would've been.

The man drew a hand from the pocket of his overalls and gave me an odd wave, fingers ticking just either side of upright, like a broken clock.

"Hello," he said, in a deepish voice and a local accent, flat vowels and a curl to the double-L.

I looked at the gate, only a dozen yards behind him. I so wanted to be through it and gone. Everything about the situation was strange: the lilac evening light, this man's sudden appearance and the way his smile churned my guts. Even the quiet was unnatural. With air so cold and clear I should have been able to hear the lads shouting on their way back into town.

Fear had crept up on me and so had the man. His second hello was right into my ear.

I don't know how he crossed the distance so quickly. He was inches away. The corduroy troughs of his jacket filled my world.

I felt fingers slip around my wrist.

Even now, I shudder thinking about it. All the horrid things you dare to touch as a boy – slugs, a dead crow, even a handful of frogspawn one time up at Reddings Lodge – none of it came close to the awfulness of his skin against mine. It was the second worst thing I've ever felt. The absolute worst would follow shortly.

I tried to pull away, but he held me fast. He might've been as thin as a racing bike, but there was strength beneath those overalls.

"Let me go!"

This was what you heard about. Little kids being taken by bad men for even worse purposes. I had an inkling of the urges involved, though it was based on the patchwork understanding of boys. The tightness of those knuckles circling my wrist, the sight of thick hair – *too thick* – peeping out from his dirty sleeves, the sheer adult mass of this man. It filled me with a black certainty. He was as wrong as wrong can be.

"Please," I squealed.

"Calm down, boy." There was a chuckle in his voice. "It's very quick."

With his other hand he opened his jacket. I saw buttons evenly spaced on the front of his overalls. Despite my terror, I thought how odd that was. I'd never seen overalls that fastened up the front. The buttons were made from a creamy ceramic that looked bright against his green fingers.

Yes, *green*, the oily tint of old beef. Purples and copper blue and even stranger colours that I'd never seen before flashed across his knuckles as he worked at the buttons.

That's when I first understood he wasn't a man.

It's a queer thing, meeting a monster. Psychologists and the people who write scary stories, they'll tell you children are malleable, that a young mind is elastic enough to stretch around the craziest things. Well, that may be true, but I felt mine come close to an almighty snap that day.

As he slipped each button free, the overalls parted. His throat and upper chest had that same murky iridescence, but every inch of exposed skin was darker than the last. No, not dark exactly, just less *bright*. I've never known how to say this, how to even picture it in my head. What's the truth of black and white again? One is all the colours. One is none, right? Well, that's what *he* was like. Everything and nothing all at once. The body below his breastbone just wasn't there. Where his stomach should have been there was a shimmering absence that looked like the outer edge of a thundercloud, solid and heavy and dark but, itself, just a caul over all the shade and depth hidden in the universe.

Under those overalls, he was a hole that looked like man.

And then he tried to force me inside.

He grabbed the back of my head and pulled me towards him. God, he was strong. I felt the muscles in my neck creak as I tried to hold myself away. My left hand was still fixed in his grip. The other I planted against a bit of his torso that was still whole. There was a smell coming out of him that stung my sinuses, like the first few minutes after a storm. Rain on hot stone, though not clean; more like a storm of stagnant water.

He drew me closer, inch by inch.

"Stop struggling, boy. We're hungry."

I heard barking again, from my left, over by the long grass. A series of frenzied, furious yips. It sounded like a puppy, and where there was a puppy there must be an owner.

"Help me." My cry was as much breath as sound.

"Shhhhhh," the man whispered. But I sensed a new urgency in his voice. As the barking grew nearer, he doubled his pressure. Now I had both hands braced against the solid edges of his body, but it was no use, I only had a dribble of strength left. My face was inches from the cavity and that squally scent blew out of him on a cold breeze. Tears froze on my cheeks.

My hand slipped. When I tried to readjust my grip, my fingers slid inside.

There's a few things I've never been able to talk about well. My best words can't grasp the sight and smell of that pit in the middle of him. But the feeling when my hand was inside him, *that* I can describe.

The cold was first. Think back to when you were a kid and you'd throw snowballs without gloves, or the pain of gripping handlebars in the winter. That's not a fraction of what true cold feels like. This was a chill that went straight through my skin and the meat of my fingers. It froze the bone. If you'd tapped my hand with a hammer, I'm sure it would have shattered like pot. The pain went even deeper

But the worst was that I could feel... *things*. Grasping things that crept forwards from the other side of that absence. 'Cos it was a tunnel, you see. It had another opening at the other end. Don't ask me how I know that. I just do. That wind had to come from somewhere.

I saw nothing, but my mind went to jellyfish. They caressed my fingers, unsure, then with a twirling and twining that burned. They wanted me enough to tug hungrily on the bits of me they could reach.

I opened my mouth to scream, but I couldn't. The disgust of that caress, the agony and insult of it, was too much.

I was done.

Then something warm pressed against my calf. Beneath my choking, I heard a growl. It began low and susurrant, then cycled up into a higher pitch. The bravest sound.

There was a click of tiny teeth, and then a sharp breath. The man took a step back and suddenly his grip on my head was gone. My hand sliding free was the most blessed relief of my life.

In any other context, what I saw would have been funny enough to make me laugh.

Between me and the man, there was a tiny dog. And I really do mean tiny. He stood no more than eight or ten inches high and the bottom of his belly barely cleared the grass. His fur was a mad scramble of gold and blond and black, with a flash of silver atop the dome of his head. A mongrel pup. The kind of scruffy mix my dad called a Heinz 57.

He was leaning forward and growling for all he was worth, lips curled back, teeth bared.

The man looked at him with horror. That appalling grin was gone.

"No, you died." There was such dismay in his voice.

The dog took a step forwards. Then another. With each the man retreated further until there was open ground between us.

"YOU DIED!" he screamed. Then, dropping his voice, "Please. Just this one. We're hungryyyyy." The word stretched to a wail.

With a snarl the puppy bounded forward, closing his jaws around a flapping trouser leg. The man stumbled backwards, crying out like he was being savaged by a lion. Of course, he was, in a way. No matter how hard he kicked out, the dog held on, whipping back and forth until I was sure his tiny spine would crack. If it did, what would happen to me? How was it that this creature seemed like my salvation?

"Let me go. Let me go." The man finally freed himself and ran for the gate. The dog was on his heels, snapping all the way, until the man turned and lashed out with a heavy boot. It sent the little body spinning and I was sure the dog must be dead.

A loud popping noise came from over by the gate, but I paid it no mind. I was too focused on the pup, who struggled to regain his feet. When he did, only three legs were working. Still, he hopped straight back into position in front of me. A high whine crept into his growl and though some of it was definitely pain, I think most of it was frustration 'cos the gate was swinging in the breeze.

The man was gone.

I scanned the walls either side of that gate, assuming he'd ducked down behind it. Panic thudded in my ears, but I had enough sense to look up and down Sheephead Lane. It was empty.

That was impossible. What is there on this stretch of Sheephead now? A bus shelter and that plant hire place? Well, back then it was even emptier, just open fields and he wasn't in any of them. There was no way he'd gotten from the gate all the way along the wall and around this corner to one of these houses either. That just wasn't possible in the few seconds he'd been out of my sight.

I was still staring up and down the lane when I felt a nuzzling under my trouser cuff. Something cold and wet touched my ankle. I thought of those tentacles and almost cried out.

The dog sat at my feet.

He whined again, and this time it was all pain.

I had no idea where this little beast had come from, why he'd defended me, or how he'd put the fear of god into a monster twenty times his size. All I knew was that that he'd saved my life and he was hurting because of it.

"Good dog."

He pressed his silver dome against my stroking hand.

I was still too full of terror to consider my other hand. The one that had gone inside. That would cause me trouble later, but right then I was most concerned with the damage done to the pup's paw. He held it up off the ground and it dangled at an awkward angle.

"Ok, boy. Ok."

There was no collar around his neck, not even twine to suggest he'd broken free of a rough leash. That means nothing, of course; it was just a boy's self-serving half-logic. There was nothing to say he didn't belong to someone who lived nearby. He was a puppy after all, and a gorgeous one at that. Nonetheless, I assumed he was a stray, and that I could keep him.

He looked up at me like he was searching my face for something he recognised.

"Do you want to come home with me, pal?"

He did that thing that dogs do: mouth open, tongue out, a big smile.

I took it as answer enough.

That's how I met Riot.

"Hang on," Margie said. "You're saying you got that dog when you were eleven?"

Jim nodded.

"Dogs don't live that long, Jim."

"Riot did."

She paused, softened her tone. "Are you sure you're not getting yourself a bit muddled. Maybe confusing Riot with another dog you had when you were a lad?"

Jim's lip twitched.

"Are you suggesting I'm dementing, Margie?"

No, she was more concerned about a schizoaffective condition. His story had all the hallmarks: hallucinations, delusions, disorganised thought. None of that made him necessarily dangerous, but Margie knew that trying to directly puncture a patient's psychosis could be like tickling a hair trigger. Risky. She wanted to proceed with as much caution as she could draw on. Though she had to admit that had never been a deep well for her.

"No, but I reckon you've had a big shock when your dog died, and if something did happen to you in that field out there – not monsters but something awful – maybe young Andy going missing has upset you more than you know. We all have senior moments, don't we? And you can't really think your dog lived almost as long as you?"

"Oh, I think he's lived a lot longer than me."

"What are you talking about?"

Jim continued.

Mam didn't notice anything was wrong with me at first. She was too angry about the dog.

"There's no way we're keeping that creature!"

She said it over and over that first week, whilst she took him to the vet and paid for his treatment, and again after she bought him food and a cheap tin dog bowl. His leg was badly sprained but not broken. With a bit of care, the vet said, it would heal perfectly well.

"We're just getting him healthy," mam said, "and then he's off to the shelter."

Dad didn't say much. He knew the likely outcome when he saw her gently applying a fresh bandage after the dog had chewed the first to ribbons.

"Stupid thing," she said, patting him on the head and giving him a treat.

After a fortnight, the bandage came off, but no one discussed what would happen next. I didn't want to say anything to remind them of our furry interloper, though I don't see how they could have forgotten. Even with his leg wrapped up, the dog quickly set about making our home his own. He would race in and out of rooms just for the joy of being alive. The living room windowsill was his favourite perch, and he'd spend hours there, watching the world and barking furiously at anyone who dared pass our house. He barely peed indoors, nor did he chew chair legs or skirting boards, so it was easy for my parents to come to terms with his presence. He really made my dad laugh, and my old man wasn't one for big shows of emotion. I think mam liked the pup for that.

Nonetheless, she refused to give the dog a name.

"No point," she said. "Whoever takes him will want to call him something else."

That didn't stop me. I tried a different name every day: Jerry and Elvis and Hank. I know I tried Vincent, 'cos I'd been a big Vincent Price fan ever since my dad snuck me in to see *The House of Usher* at the Eureka. Great film but a terrible name for the dog. It was too stately for such a hurtling creature. As a puppy, he was as chaotic as a drum kit being kicked downstairs.

Then one evening as mam was serving up tea, he came bursting into the kitchen so fast that his paws lost purchase on the linoleum. There was a scrabble of claws as he tried to bank, slid sideways through mam's legs, and went crashing into the cupboards. All three of us recoiled at the thought of his injured leg.

He had no such worries. Just righted himself and tore off out of the room, stubby tail high and proud.

"That bloody dog is a one-man riot," my mam said.

It stuck. I started calling him Riot, then my dad joined in, and by the end of that weekend mam was using his name as she laid out his food. The cheap tin had been replaced by a thick pot bowl with the words 'Good Boy' stamped into the clay. Mam claimed she'd got it for free when she'd taken Riot back to the vet for a check-up, but it had the new sheen of something shop-bought.

With that, Riot's place in our house was cemented. No one ever acknowledged it, but any talk of giving him away had stopped. Mam still called him *that bloody dog*, but she loved him as much as any of us. Most nights, after tea, when we all sat down to watch *Coronation Street* – remember when that was new? – he'd either crawl to her or she'd gather him up, and they'd sit together on the settee until one of them fell asleep.

Riot adored my mam and dad. He pined for weeks when they died. But it was me he loved most. From the day I carried him home, wrapped in my jacket, we were inseparable. If I was elsewhere in the house he'd pad around to find me, and when I went to school, my mam said he sat in the front window and howled until she had to stop what she was doing and cuddle him. Eventually she made him a cushion out of an old jumper of mine to calm him until I came home. Over the years I've heard people ask the question, what's the one thing you'd tell your dog if you could talk to them? Most people choose *I love you*, but that's a waste 'cos dogs already know that. I'd have told Riot that he didn't have to worry when I was gone. That I'd always come back.

And I always did.

My parents only asked once about how Riot came into our lives. I told them I'd found him up the Square with his bad leg. They believed me, 'cos it was basically the truth.

I didn't tell them about the man. I didn't know how.

Supposedly, a lot of kids who have bad things happen to them – nasty abuse, sexual stuff – they don't tell people 'cos they feel ashamed. Shame might seem daft from an adult's perspective, but as a youngster you don't always know how the world works. You don't know what the rules are, or the consequences of honesty. My dad would have been straight out to find anyone who'd tried it on with me, and god knows what he'd have done.

But how would they have reacted if I told them my story? I didn't want my parents to think I was mad. The thought of their faces creasing at the realisation that they had a fantasist for a child. No, I didn't even know where to start. So I just kept quiet. I won't say there weren't nightmares, 'cos I had plenty. For weeks I jolted out of sleep like someone pulled the ripcord to my heart. I'd lie there, charged with alarm, part of thinking I'd been pushed all the way into that darkness. It was easy to imagine those *things* reaching for me, oily fronds inches away and coming closer, always a half-second from my bare skin. There are nights now when I wake up and for a second I'm still eleven and I'm about to die.

Riot rescued me every night. During those awful three-in-the-morning spasms, he'd rouse himself from his spot between my knees, lick my face – the sandpaper comfort of his tongue nothing like those lapping tentacles – and he'd lay down with his head on my chest. He was a warm anchor to the real world.

So, it was ok. Life went on. If my parents knew about my nightmares, they didn't mention them to me.

They did notice my hand though. That was hard to miss.

I hadn't thought about it immediately. Riot's paw took precedence, but after I got into the house and endured mam's first bout of yelling about bringing a stray home, that's when I felt it. Not pain so much as that sensation somewhere between numbness and hurt, like the raw gum around a loose tooth. There were no wounds though – just troughs where the skin had wrinkled and slackened. It's gotten much worse as I've aged, but even then, that first day, it already looked like an old man's hand.

I held it out to Riot, who sniffed it suspiciously. When he finally ran his tongue across that weird patch of skin, it felt absurdly like an all-clear.

Still, mam spotted it.

She first mentioned it the morning after when we were eating breakfast. My fingers felt swollen and clumsy and I kept dropping my knife. She demanded to know what was wrong and I almost made up a story about spilled chemicals at school. Then realised that would end with her berating poor Mr Brackstone, our addled chemistry teacher, come Monday morning. Instead, I told her I'd fallen in a patch of nettles.

"It doesn't look right," she said.

"Maybe he's allergic," my dad offered.

"Did that dog bite you?" She glared at Riot, who was sitting by my chair, already comfortable in his new surroundings.

I assured her he hadn't and that my hand was fine, but she insisted we get it checked.

"You never know what creepy crawlies are knocking about these days. Last week I read in the paper about some spider that came over on a banana boat. Bit a woman's hand when she bought a bunch. She nearly lost it."

I wanted to tell her that whatever stung me wasn't a spider, and it came from somewhere much further away than wherever they grew bananas.

Doctor Holt was fascinated by the rash. He turned my hand back and forth under his desk lamp, peered it at through a magnifying glass, and even took a fine scraping of skin into a Petri dish.

"I've never seen the like," he said. "The boy's hand looks prematurely geriatric."

"What does that mean?" Mam asked.

"It means it looks old, Mrs Howarth."

I recognised the particular twist of her lips. Uh oh, I thought. Don't speak down to her.

"I know what geriatric means, Doctor." She was all clipped tones now. "I mean, what does it mean for James' hand?"

Doc Holt was unsure. He mentioned some disease that made little kids look like old people, but he said that would've started when I was a toddler.

"Tell me, Mrs Howarth, has the boy been near anything that emits radiation?"

Mam looked at him over her glasses. I knew that look, too.

"Sorry, Doctor, do you think I've been taking him up to Windscale at the weekend?"

"Not at all," he chuckled. "It's just that cellular decay of that type would generally require a rather large dose of radiation. Especially, as you say, it happened very quickly."

She nodded. "Overnight. One day he had a perfectly smooth hand. The next, all these wrinkles. He says it was a nettle sting, but I tell you," she was ramping up now, "if it turns out that our James has been poisoned, I'll sue the council for all they're worth."

Doctor Holt assured us both, if that were the case, I'd have other symptoms to worry about, none of which I was exhibiting. He also asked if I could come back for more tests. He mentioned papers he could author and lots of tests, all the while looking greedily at my hand like it was pointing his way to fame. Mam noticed my discomfort.

"Let's see how he gets on," she said. "If it gets any worse, I'll be sure to bring him back."

We shuffled out of the surgery, Doc Holt's entreaties about the need for further study chasing us all the way to the street.

"Well," she said, when we reached the pavement, "I hope you haven't been messing with any Soviet rockets, Jim."

For the hundredth time I tiptoed right up to the cusp of telling her what had happened, but she looked so relieved. If something as far-fetched as radiation was the only thing the doctor could think of, it meant she had no sensible reason to worry. What kind of son would spoil that by telling her I'd rubbed up against something that broke sensible in half?

"No, mam. Just nuclear nettles."

She laughed; a full head-tipper. I loved it when I could make that happen. Three years later she'd be dead and there was much less laughter in my life for a time. But when I think of my mam, I sometimes see her cracking up in the cold sunshine outside the doctor's surgery, laughing 'cos there was nothing wrong with her boy, or at least she let herself believe so. I'm glad I didn't ruin that. In some ways I'm glad she didn't have to see what became of my life. She had such dreams for me. She wouldn't have understood.

"Let's get home," she said. "See what that bloody dog is up to."

"What did she die of?"

"Cancer," Jim replied. "Ovarian."

"I'm sorry. You were what...?"

"Fourteen."

"Hard age for a boy to lose his mother."

"Hmm."

"So, it was just you and your dad?"

"Aye, and he was a good 'un. Never knocked me about. Never turned to the drink or lost his job. Always kept us fed. He kept the ship sailing, even in those first years after she went."

"So, what did happen to your hand?" Curiousity had taken Margie by the arm once again.

"I told you, it was those things."

"The tentacles inside the man?"

"Aye."

Margie decided to go with it. She could butt heads with Jim all evening, but if she wanted to know what he knew about Andy Hoyle, she had the feeling the best way forward was to follow the delusions, and hope they led somewhere sane.

"What are you thinking, Jim?"

"What I've always wondered. Whether those things are part of him, or something else that lives wherever that hole inside him leads? Whatever they are, he keeps them tucked away. Every other time I've seen him, he just looked like a man. A strange man."

"*Other* times?" Margie coughed out a mouthful of tepid tea.

"Oh, aye. Riot and me, we've had a good few meetings with that bastard. We've worked hard keeping him at bay."

"Keeping him at—"

Jim just rolled over her.

"Riot knew what we were supposed to do right from the start. Every time we went for a walk he'd pull towards Sheephead Lane. At first I thought maybe he was trying to go back home, and it made me a bit sad 'cos I wanted to keep him for myself. But even when I knew why he was so intent on coming up here, I still denied him. I was bloody scared of this bit of land and I swore I'd never come back up here."

"So, what brought you?"

"Riot eventually. But first..." Jim trailed off.

"First?"

"That thing took Emily Lumb."

Emily was a nice girl. She smiled easy and often, and she had this great, gravelly laugh that you couldn't help but join in with. Add blonde hair and a tan and Emily

Lumb was the closest thing any of us had seen to a girl off the American telly.

She went missing two days before Valentine's Day.

Katherine took Emily's disappearance the hardest. The two of them were joined at the hip since primary school and, though she was half-mad with worry for her friend, she still had to field everyone's questions. It was the kids asking the questions, but you could tell it was their mams and dads who really wanted the answers.

Is it true she was pregnant?

I heard she ran away with a married bloke.

Weren't you the last one to see her?

The truth, as Katherine told me later, is that yes, she was the last person to see Emily alive. She didn't put it that way – I don't think Katherine ever truly accepted that Emily was dead – but the two of them had been together on the afternoon she vanished.

'Cos it was so close to Valentine's day, people got the idea that Emily had done a runner with a secret boyfriend, or she'd met up with someone who wasn't to be trusted. Katherine was adamant that she'd have known about it. They kept no secrets from each other.

There was no boyfriend. Not one who loved her, nor one who went mad and murdered her.

How do I know?

Have a guess where Katherine saw Emily for the last time?

Aye.

Emily lived up here. If you go a bit further up Sheephead, away from town, there's a few old quarrymen's cottages set back from the road. Her and her mam rented one of those.

Katherine told me she often met Emily at the Square after school for a smoke. That day as they came out to the lane and said their see-you-laters, Emily realised she'd left her schoolbag near the swings.

That old swing set was just where the current one is now at the top of the Square. It should only have taken half a minute for Emily to dash back, collect her bag, and be off home. So, Katherine did nothing wrong in setting off home herself. It's important to say that 'cos the guilt always chewed at her.

I wanted to tell her that it wasn't her fault. That I was glad she left when she did.

I said nothing, though. Not to anyone. What was I going to do, go down to the police station and report that a monster had eaten Emily Lumb? That she was under the floorboards of the universe with the cosmic jellyfish?

There was no evidence of anything untoward. Just a schoolbag left sitting by the swings. Like with this new lad: Andy and his football. No sign at all of a struggle, not a shred of clothing or a drop of blood. Nothing to suggest that Emily hadn't just walked away.

The police looked for her for a few weeks, at a slackening pace, and then they just stopped. Remember, this was the early sixties. A lot of kids were getting fed up with living 'round here. When you saw Manchester and London on the telly, it might have been in black and white, but that still looked a lot better than all this grey.

Emily's mam, Barbara, she tried to keep interest alive, but it always fades eventually. As much as anything she got tired and ashamed of what people said about her daughter. That laugh of Emily's, people started remembering it differently to how it sounded. Not bright but dirty. An invitation to improper things. Or worse, a sign of her getting above her station.

As I've gotten older, I've come to see that's the worst thing you can be in Symester: above your station. We rip holes in each other 'round here. Anyone wants to stand a bit taller to see a bit more of the world, they're liable to get their legs kicked from under them.

The weeks after Emily went missing were a strange time for me. Of course I was reeling from what had happened to me, and what I knew had happened to her. What a weight that was for an eleven-year-old. Without Riot I don't think I could have borne it. But I did have him, and as mad as it might sound, all things considered, I was happy.

That dog brought cheer into our house when we were in sore need of it. We'd buried my grandad the previous October and the long winter nights had been a lid, bottling my mam in with her grief. The promise of spring played its part in brightening her mood, but Riot did more. He uncorked us all. His puny fury when a tennis ball rolled under the furniture; his clumsy attempts to navigate the stairs; the way he could sleep *anywhere*. One time we couldn't find him and turned the house upside down, only to discover him curled up in an empty plant pot outside.

Riot reminded us that there were things to laugh about. To a grownup it would have been a poor counterweight to the horror I'd seen, but at eleven, it balanced off fine.

If I'd known the price I'd pay for bringing Riot home, would I still have done it? I really don't know. In my worst moments I've cursed him as a burden, but he's not to blame. He just did what he was sent here to do, and I'm not sure he could have done it without me. That's not self-importance, just practicality, 'cos he was so small. Far too small to hold the heart that he had.

And I loved him. If he was the hinge between what my life was and what it could've been, then so be it.

There were other turning points, too. The next was when I overheard Mr Cuddy and my dad telling their ghost stories.

George Cuddy was a widower from up our street. His wife had died a few weeks after my grandad and he'd had a bad winter of it. When my mam invited him over for tea I usually tried to make myself scarce 'cos the old bloke loved nothing more than talking about Symester history. At eleven it's hardly scintillating, hearing about quarrying and farming and disputes that started half a century before you were born. These days I'm just as bad as he was. It seeps into you, this fascination with the past. When you get old you suddenly feel you've got more in common with those who are long gone than with a lot of people still here. It makes sense 'cos the dead are just the other side of a single missed breath. Whereas the young are a lifetime away.

After we'd eaten, Mam put two bottled ales on the kitchen table and took herself off to the living room. She'd been kind to George and cooked for him, but she didn't feel any obligation to listen to him natter. George and my dad settled into conversation and I let it burble over me as I washed the pots. I would've fled the room myself shortly after, if not for a snatch of sentence.

"—just like that Lumb girl. Not the first, won't be the last."

I stopped my scrubbing and tuned in.

"Oh, come on George," my dad said, kindly. "There's no such thing."

"No such thing, young Stephen?" (He always called my dad that.) "I tell you I saw it."

"Saw it?"

"Aye. The boggart. Nasty bugger. Looks like a man, but it's not."

My dad picked up George's bottle and pretended to examine it.

"Are you drinking stronger beer than me, old timer?"

From where I was standing by the sink, I could see my dad's eyes twitch to me. He gave a half-smile. The only part of George I could see was the back of his neck, which had bloomed red between his yellowed collar and an unkempt widower's thatch.

"I'm telling you, young Stephen!" He shook a finger in my dad's face. "That bloody thing has been the bane of this valley for a *long* time." He stretched out the word long.

"A boggart?"

"*The* boggart. There's only one. Or only one in these parts, anyhow. Nasty bugger. Takes kids. Always has."

My dad's smile melted.

"George, it's a serious business. There's a young girl missing—"

"Aye and, like I say, she won't be the last. It's a hungry bugger."

My dad decided I'd heard enough.

"Go see how your mam is, Jim. See if she needs anything."

I tried to protest, desperate to hear more, but my dad was having none of it.

"Go on, Jim. Now."

Sulkily, I dried my hands and crossed the room.

Riot got up from his slump by my dad's feet and wound his way through a maze of chair and human legs to join me. George looked my way. Whether to bid me goodnight or countermand my dad's orders, I don't know, but his eyes landed on Riot and I saw him do a double take.

"That your pup, young Jim?"

"Yes, Mr Cuddy."

"Smart looking dog. Got some Jack Russell in him, I reckon. Scared of nowt, are they?" He clicked his tongue. "Come here, boy."

Riot ambled over to meet the outstretched finger. He licked it once then settled with pleasure as George stroked back and forth over the silver splash of fur atop the dog's head.

"Sign of a prince."

"What is, Mr Cuddy?"

"This crown of his." He turned to me with a funny look on his face. "You keep this dog close to you, son. He's a good 'un. He'll keep you safe. Like I say, he's scared of nothing."

"Ok. Now, Jim. Off you go." My dad's voice was firm.

I nodded goodnight to them both, called Riot and together we left the room. Through the closing door I heard my dad remonstrating with George about what he'd said in front of me.

"You think what you like, young Stephen," George replied. "But if I were you I'd keep your boy close and tell him to keep that dog closer."

Anything else they had to say was cut off with the click of the jamb.

It took me a week to gather the courage to go see Mr Cuddy. When you're very young the elderly are frightening in a way that you can't fully articulate. I was scared of him telling me to buzz off or reporting to my dad that I'd been bothering him. I was also wary of finding out things that would further disturb my still-settling sleep. But, beyond all that, I think I was most frightened of George Cuddy's loneliness. I'd only been in his house once before, in the aftermath of his wife's death, when my mam managed to unbury herself from her own grief long enough to help assuage his with hot dinners.

Even then, with Mrs Cuddy only dead a few days, his house had felt stuffy with old man sorrow. Clothes sagged from the back of chairs, the kitchen bin was overflowing with tins, and a heavy fog of fried food hung in the air. It was a house of abandonment, and how much worse would it be after he'd spent a full winter alone? I decided to take Riot with me. He had impressed George, and I thought he might soften the annoyance of a kid knocking on his door in the middle of the day. Riot charged ahead, snorting and chuffing on a tight lead.

He was always eager for a walk, but this was another level of excitement. Usually, we turned left out of our gate, down Darwin street, towards the canal banking, but this time we'd turned right, up the hill towards George's house.

Towards Sheephead Lane and towards the Square.

"Whoa, boy. You're going to choke yourself."

As small as he was, he pulled with real power, every muscle churning him forward.

When we reached George's front door he didn't want to stop. I had to yank him back violently to get him to heel. He looked up at me with shiny pebble eyes and I felt immediately guilty.

"Sorry, Riot. We're not going up there. I've told you."

I tussled his head and he gave me a quick lick as if to say *ok, still friends*. But there was an intensity growing in him. An impatience. I don't know if it was instinct or some higher reasoning, but Riot knew where he was supposed to go and what he was supposed to do. I was the coward holding him back.

I worry about that sometimes: how long it took me to gather the courage, especially after Emily.

But I was only a boy, I tell myself. Only a scared boy.

"Now, be good."

I swear that dog rolled his eyes at me.

"What?" I said. "We're here, aren't we?"

Checking each way, on the off chance either of my parents were in the street, I knocked on the door.

A half-minute passed and I was about to knock again, or maybe just go home, when I saw movement through the dirty net curtains.

"Who is it?" George called through the door.

In the delay between his question and my answer, there was another chance at a different life. I almost took it, almost sped off and tried to convince myself I was just playing knock-a-door-run. I didn't though.

Curiosity and fear are two faces of the same bastard fate.

"It's James Howarth, Mr Cuddy."

I heard the scrabble of a chain being unhooked and then the door was drawn open to reveal a shaky sketch of the man who'd been at my house the week before.

Though it was the middle of the day, George wore a dressing gown scabbed with egg yolk. He was poorly shaven and there was a noticeable smell of something stronger than beer coming off him.

He fixed me with a firm stare.

"Ah, young Jim." He cleared his throat. "I thought you'd be 'round to see me. Does your dad know you're here?"

I could've lied, but I think he'd have known and sent me packing.

"No, sir."

"Probably for the best." He glanced down the street. "Is that dog of yours house trained?"

"Yes."

He really was. Aside from a few incidents he'd quickly got to grips with toilet etiquette. He'd just quietly go to the back door and sit. My dad hadn't even had to rub his nose in his mess.

"Alright then. Come in."

George held the door open and I shuffled inside, trying not inhale the funk of unwashed cotton as I passed under his arm. Riot trotted happily at my heels. It was only when I got into the front room that I realised George hadn't even asked why I'd disturbed him.

Of course, he knew.

He flopped into his armchair and gestured to its threadbare twin.

"Sit down, son."

The chair was cluttered with the leavings of a solitary life: newspapers and magazines, a pile of dishcloths, plenty of the types of brown paper bags that my dad carried home from the pub on a Friday night. Embarrassed, I tried to make room for myself.

"Oh, just shove it to one side. I've no time for tidying up. Doris used to do all of that." He rubbed at his temple. "Just ask me what you've come to ask me."

Now the moment had come I froze up.

At my house, George was boring at best, stern at worst. Here, he was an old bear in his den, irritable at being roused from hibernation.

"Well? Go on!"

"The other night, Mr Cuddy, you were talking to my dad about something."

"Aye lad. What of it?"

"Well, it's just that... a few weeks back..."

I trailed off. My breath had gone short and, out of nowhere, I felt a prickle build behind my eyes.

Gently, Riot stretched to lick my dangling hand. It shored me enough to lurch on.

"I saw it Mr Cuddy, earlier this year. The thing that took Emily Lumb, it tried... it tried to take me as well."

"Were he grey?"

The speed of George's question surprised me. Despite the things he'd said to my dad, I'd half expected him to laugh me out of his house, or at least to require some convincing.

"WERE he all in GREY?" Half-shouting now.

"Yes," I said.

"And smiling? A big beaming grin, like the cat who got all of his own cream and most of yours."

"Yes."

George steepled his fingers beneath his nose, muffling his next question. I think he wanted to pretend he wasn't asking what he was asking.

"Did he show you himself? Did he show you what he were made of?"

"Yes." I was almost sobbing now, the memory of that chasm in the man, in the universe, all the terror of it slammed back into me for the first time in my waking life.

"And what were he made of, young Jim?"

"Holes."

It was the right answer, the key to a lock that opened George up like a well-stocked pantry.

"Oh, good god in heaven," he said.

There was horror in his words but also relief.

Now, sitting here myself, an old man telling you my story, I understand him better. I confirmed for George that he wasn't mad. How long had he held on to what he knew, or thought he knew, over the years? It's a terrible thing to be lashed to a secret all your life. I should know.

"Have you seen him, Mr Cuddy?"

He let out a long, shivery breath and sat back in his chair.

"Aye, son. I saw him. I saw him when he tried to take my kid brother. Will were only nine and if it hadn't been for—" He broke off and stared at Riot, who'd crossed the room to nuzzle against the old man's bare calf.

"Where did you get this dog, Jim?"

"Up at the Square."

"The same day that you met that thing?"

I nodded.

He bent forward and picked Riot up. The dog gave a surprised yip but seemed happy with his place in George's lap.

"Look at you, little 'un." Again, George stroked the silver patch on Riot's head. "Where did you get this, I wonder?" Riot's eyes went dim with pleasure.

"You were saying about your brother, Mr Cuddy?"

He struggled to pull his attention from my dog.

"Aye. Will were up there with his pals that afternoon. When he didn't come home, mother sent me up to fetch him."

"He was up at the Square?" I asked.

"Aye, lads and lasses have always played up there. Aside from them few houses you've got the place to yourself, haven't you. It's a good place to play. But it's a fair way from town, so by the time I got up there, it were going dark."

"Purple," I said, unbidden.

George gave me a knowing look. "Purple, that's right. That funny light when the night's peeking over the hills. It were just about that time when I got there."

"What did you see?"

"Our Will were on his own. His mates had just left him up there. I gave each of them a good hiding in the next week or so, you believe me. But Will were standing in the middle of that bloody field and I were about to shout to him from over the wall, but just when I opened my mouth, I saw it.

"The man?"

"Aye, least, I thought he were a man then, too. He were standing between the gate and our Will, with his back to me. Dressed all in grey like a smear against the evening. And then he just walked right up and grabbed hold of our kid. He were always a bit of a daft lad, our Will, but I couldn't believe how he just stood there with his mouth hung open like he were trying to catch flies."

I remembered how pinned I'd felt as the man had approached me. If it hadn't been for Riot's first bark pulling my attention away, would I have stood there slack and dopey until he took me?

"Then, the boggart – 'cos that's what he is, you take my word for it – he starts messing around with his clothes and I start shouting, 'cos mother had warned me and Will about men like him. Men like I thought he were."

There was a ragged edge in George's voice now.

"I saw Will see me, and he came back into himself. Started struggling but he were too little to free himself. I were half over the wall, but what were I going to do, not much beyond your age, and no size myself?" George smiled, absently. "My Doris always said that the nicest things come in the smallest boxes. Lucky for me, I guess."

"Did you fight him, Mr Cuddy?"

"No, son. I'd like to say I did, but it weren't me that saved our Will. It were a dog."

I turned still as stone. George smirked, like he knew a secret I'd yet to learn.

"Collie dog it were. Huge bugger, all matted and dirty. It came out of the trees down the bottom end of the Square. There used to be a nice patch of oaks down there, but they all got cut down during the war. The army probably needed the wood. Anyway, this mutt, up it comes, I were as worried about it going for Will as much as anything."

George smiled again. He gave Riot's head a playful shake.

"Good boy."

Riot just grinned up at him, then at me as if to say: *Aren't I lucky that everyone thinks I'm wonderful?*

"The boggart just dropped my brother like a hot coal. Bugger only just managed to get his hands up in front of him before the dog hit him. If it'd got its teeth round him, I think it would've killed him dead, if such things can be killed. As it were, the boggart went right on his arse and the dog snarled him all the way out the gate."

"Did you see where he went?" I asked, remembering how swiftly the man had disappeared after Riot had chased him off.

"No. It were the damndest thing. By the time I'd checked on our Will, that thing were nowhere to be seen. It were just us and the dog."

"What did the dog do? Did you take it home."

"Pshht, not a chance. It looked half-savage and my father would likely have shot it. That Collie just gave our Will a serious stare like it were warning him to stay away. Then it sloped off back to those trees.

"Was Will ok?"

"Aye, of a sort. He had nightmares for months after. He'd wake up screaming and at first, our father was patient. Then, after a while Will got a crack when he woke the house up. From then on I'd hear him lying there across the room, trying not to cry. I wish I'd gone to him, given him a hug. But lads don't, do they?"

George's face went stiff with old shame.

"I only really asked Will about it once, and he told me about how that horrible bugger smiled, and how he were empty inside. That when he opened his shirt there were nowt there but nothing. *He wanted me to fall inside him.* That's how our kid described it. *He wanted me to fall into the monsters.*"

Shaken, George turned back to me.

"Is that what you saw?" he asked.

"Yes, sir."

"And this little one rescued you?" He ruffled Riot's fur.

"Yes. Just like your dog."

"Hmm. It weren't ever my dog, young Jim, though I saw it about over the years. Over a lot of years, come to think of it." He gave me a funny look. "Do you know the one thing I haven't told you yet?"

"What's that, Mr Cuddy?"

"That Collie, right between its ears, it had a shiny bright patch of silver."

We looked at each other in silence.

Riot turned his head from one of us to the other, wondering why the stroking had stopped.

*

Margie took a sip of whisky and weighed her doubts. Everything about the story was lunacy, but she couldn't help seeing truth in Jim's hunched shoulders, his grimacing awareness of how it all sounded. That's why she'd fetched the bottle.

"So, you're telling me that George's Collie and your Riot, they're related or something?"

"No," he said. "I think they're the same thing."

"What?" Margie's tongue snapped on the word. Why did this man feel the need to keep pushing her?

"Whatever that Collie was, something of it is in Riot."

"Reincarnation now? Oh, come on!"

Jim shrugged.

"I don't know anything for certain, Margie. I only know what George told me, and what he showed me."

"Showed you?"

"Oh, aye, he showed me plenty. Enough to keep me stuck here all these years." He shrugged. "Do you want to see for yourself?"

"Will I end up trapped here, too?" Margie chuckled. She was sixty-seven years old and she didn't envisage much escaping in her future. Symester had been home for forty years, this house for almost half of that. She'd lived here, loved here, even done a fair amount of laughing here, and she fully expected she'd die here. There were worse places.

"Fine," she said. "Show me."

He lumbered to his feet and limped to the back door, waving away her protestations about his knee. For a second Margie thought he was leaving, that maybe she'd called his bluff. But slowly, with evident pain, he bent to the holdall.

"What are you doing, Jim?"

"It's all in here," he said. "I'm going to bury it with him. Now he's gone, I want rid of all of it."

Jim reached gently into the bag.

"I'm sorry, boy," he whispered. "Don't mind me. You sleep."

He returned to the table with a plastic envelope. When he tipped it a wad of paper slid out in a tidy spray of typeface.

"George gave me a lot of this, but I've added my own findings over the years."

Margie fanned the clippings out across the table. There were dozens, some of them yellowed and curled, with ragged edges where they'd been torn free of their page. Most were more recently photocopied, though their contents ranged from newspaper font to a florid, handwritten scrawl. It was such a barrage of text that Margie struggled to make sense of any of it, until a particular headline hooked her eye.

Douglas Boy Taken, Sister Cries 'Monster'

It was the front page of the *Free Press*, dated November 8th, 1902. The story reported the abduction

of ten-year-old Albert Douglas on the afternoon of the
Fifth, when he and his twin sister, Francis, were col-
lecting wood for that evening's bonfire. Margie prickled
when she read that the children "encountered their foe
on a piece of recreational ground, commonly known
hereabouts as the Square".

She scanned the narrow columns of text, marvelling
at how closely the details corresponded to the stories
Jim had told her. The twins had been confronted in
the late afternoon by a figure who "snatched Albert up
in his heavy, dour woollens and absconded with him".
The reporter wrote that "the bereft sister is adamant
that they were accosted neither by known assailant, nor
by unknown actor but that her brother fell prey to a
horrid creature in the guise of a man".

Though Francis' testimony was dismissed as "child-
like misconstructions", the report did acknowledge the
area's long history of legend and tragedy, pointing to the
name of the site and referencing a similar disappearance
decades prior. It ended by asking whether there "could
be any veracity to the persistent rumours of unnatural
encounter and baffling vanishment that place a blemish
upon this corner of our pleasant valley?"

"Long-winded bugger, isn't he?" Jim said.

Margie barely heard him as she rifled through the
fragments. There were so many. A sidebar from the
paper in March 1889 noted that two fairground work-
ers had been scared "half to the afterlife by an unnatural figure haunting the edges of their campground".
It didn't surprise Margie to discover where the fair

had pitched up. An ancient church pamphlet entreated parishioners to "pray together for the vanquishment of goblins, boggarts and bogies in our good and Godly valley", whilst an unsourced illustration showed children fleeing a long-legged, spiderish figure with far too many teeth in its mouth. Beneath the picture someone had written in sharp, cursive, *is this what took our Sam?*

As she was about to push the illustration aside, she noticed a detail in the lower half of the picture. Between the terrified children and the thing in pursuit, the artist had sketched a dog. It was small and black and its teeth were bared in challenge.

She couldn't resist a glance at Jim. He had the studiedly neutral expression of someone trying not to say I told you so.

Next, she came to a crumbling page of a book titled, *Rural Speech and Folk-lore of Lancashire*. In the first paragraph the author defined a boggart as "a diabolic and solitary sprite, native to the bogs, cloughs and moorland of the East Pennines". Though they allowed that the entity was thought to roam further afield, there seemed to be little consensus on what the thing actually *was*. Collected descriptions ranged from humanoid figures to "squat, shaggy, hobgoblins" and even, in one case near Clitheroe, something invisible that sounded more like a poltergeist. Boggart, it seemed, was just the name that every little town in the northwest gave to their night terrors.

To Margie, all of this research was a key indication of secondary delusion. Any half-decent psychiatrist would look at this table and see it as a life spent fishing for information that Jim could use as scaffolding for his paranoia, and a grandiose paranoia at that.

But a few things did track. In almost all the collected legends boggarts were notorious for stealing children, and they were typically associated with a single site. The author listed several: Boggart Hole Clough, Townley Bridge, Hackensall Hall, and Symester's Bogie Square.

"When was this written?" she asked.

"Early eighteen hundreds. I've tried to hunt down the full book but no luck."

Jim slid a single clipping out of the mess.

"Read this one."

It was an A4 printout from *The Journal of Folklore Research*, the Winter 1996 edition.

The article in question was written by a Professor Glennis Stoker and on any other day the title alone would have sent Margie looking for the telly control.

"'Daemonic Topographies: The Anti-Genius Loci in the Folkloric Traditions of Northern England'. Are you taking the mick, Jim? You want me to read this?"

"Not all of it. It's a bit dry."

"Really? 'Cos it sounds a right laugh."

"I can sum it up," Jim said. "Stoker basically argues that the ancient Roman tradition of the genius loci..." he paused. "Do you know what that is?"

Margie stared a hole in him. "No, Jim. I've been a bit too busy to keep up with my Roman traditions. Washing and ironing, y'know. Bandaging daft old men's knees."

He wasn't deterred. "It means 'spirit of place'. The idea is that some sites have entities, like nymphs or dryads, good spirits who are tied to that place as protectors or guardians. These days they're mostly seen as old ways of thinking about nature, early conservation efforts with a story attached. Stoker sees it differently. According to her, these genius loci were very real, and they were the enemies of something just as real."

"She sounds barking mad."

"Well, I think a lot of her colleagues probably agree with you, 'cos as far as I'm aware that paper was the last thing she ever published. Knowing what I know, I take her more seriously. She found evidence all over the world. Statues and pottery and mosaics all showing scenes of these things having a scrap. Here, look."

Jim flipped through the stapled pages until he reached a photograph of a squat stone column. A sharp finlike edge protruded from the top.

"A sundial?" she asked.

"Aye, from the Valley of the Kings. In Egypt."

It was a grainy reproduction, but Margie could still see the intricately carved designs that decorated the dial. To the right of the vertical noonday shadow was an artist's rendition of a great cat, rearing up, front paws ready to strike. Facing it across the shadow line was an ugly mixture of man and many-headed serpent.

"That's Apep," Jim said. "Or Apophis. This great evil of Ancient Egypt, or so they say."

"Sounds scary. Ugly bugger for sure. So, he's their boggart, is he?"

"Aye," Jim said, pleased. "That's just what Stoker thinks he is, in his way. She thinks that he was something that once haunted that one site, fighting that cat, and that over time his legend spread."

"But not the cat's legend?"

"When do heroes ever get the credit they deserve, Margie? Riot never will. And anyway, those Egyptians loved their moggies, didn't they? Maybe that one cat is the reason why."

"But why are you showing me a sundial from Egypt, Jim?"

"Because of this."

He flipped the page to reveal another photo. This one was of a rough stone – limestone if she had to guess – and at the centre was a design strikingly similar to that on the sundial. A curving line cut the stone in two, with a hound, or maybe a wolf, on one side, and on the other, something harder to pin down. Not a hybrid this time but a thin humanoid shape with waving line snaking from the torso. A ragged curve was carved across the head, extending beyond the edges of the face.

Like a too-wide smile.

"And look." Jim pointed to the notation, and Margie felt her mouth fall open.

The Syme Stone, discovered July 1818, at the base of a drystone wall in Symester, Lancashire.

"They dug it up just out there," he said. "When they were bedding in the lane. Some people think it's a Danish runestone, though the Danes didn't have much presence in the valley. Stoker thinks it's much older, 'cos of something to do with the chiselling. I don't really understand that part. Either way it's—"

Margie held up a hand to quiet him. She kept it in the air as she poured them both a fresh dram and took a sizeable mouthful.

"Let me see if I've got this right, Jim. This boggart, you think it's been haunting that field for centuries?"

"Aye."

"And you think it took Andy Hoyle?"

"Aye."

"And your dog – who you say you've have had since you were eleven – is some kind of guardian angel that's kept it away all these years?"

"Well, I might not say *angel*. Most of the time he was anything but!" A sad chuckle. "But aye."

"And the dog comes back again and again?"

Jim flipped between the pictures of the sundial and the stone and pointed to the detail she'd missed. In both images the other creature – the roaring cat, the canine, the thing she was already thinking of as The Guardian – had a minor detail carved into its head. On the cat it was a small circle, easily interpreted as a third eye. On the dog or wolf, it was clearly diamond shaped.

Don piped up for the first time since Jim began his story.

It's just coincidence, love.

Margie tried to listen to her husband's old, tame rationality, but this didn't look like coincidence; like two carvings made centuries and continents apart, sharing features not only with each other but with the very same animal that lay in a bag on her kitchen floor.

That's when Jim took a fold of white card from his wallet. Margie guessed what it was going to be before he unfolded it, but still she felt a thrill of wonder when he did.

There, in tea-stained sepia, was a young man, of no more than eighteen or twenty. He didn't look exactly like the tired specimen sitting across from her, but she thought that, were she able to smooth out his creases, much of the boy would reveal himself. In the photo he was sitting on a doorstep. He had an arm around a woman whose beauty was only partially obscured by the motion blur as she threw her head back to laugh. They were both laughing.

In the space between their touching knees, there was a dog. Lolling tongue, bright, beady eyes full of fire and joy, with that white diamond patch above them.

"That's you, is it?" she asked

"Aye. Summer of 1969. The day after we went to the moon."

"And that's Riot, I expect."

"Aye."

Margie exhaled. Took a sip of her whisky.

"Ok then, Jim. I'll bite. What have you two been up to all these years?"

*

We patrolled.

Every day for sixty-odd years we walked round that field, and all that time we kept that thing from taking anyone else. Until that poor little boy on Sunday. Riot passed on Saturday afternoon, so the boggart took the first chance it got. That's what I've always been afraid of, but it makes sense. It must have been starving.

But I'm getting ahead of myself, aren't I?

Three years passed between that afternoon in George's front room and the day we took up our watch. That's how I've always thought of it, as our duty, to watch over this bloody awful town. But I was only eleven when George told me what he knew, and whilst that made it easier to believe my dog was magic, it also meant that I didn't have a clue what to do about it.

You have to understand how little *I* understand about any of this, even now. The newspapers, the old books, George's story, even my own: it's all just edges of the picture. I've no idea why it takes children, or where that hole in itself leads to. All I know is that after Emily, nothing happened, then kept not happening. It makes me think that when that thing feasts, it stays full for a while.

Course, it could be just that most of us avoided the Square. Obviously, I had my reasons for not wanting to go up there, but it didn't take much to convince the other lads to play football elsewhere. We believed Katherine, and for us the Square was spoiled ground. Perhaps that's what happens every time a kid gets taken: the rest of that generation shies away, until eventually they forget, or shrink it all to a childhood story they once believed. But they don't go back to play there. That thing has to wait for the next lot, who don't know enough to be afraid.

But then the bad thing happened to Herbie Booth's little brother in December 1964, and I knew that my head-in-the-sand time was running out.

No one really knows what befell Bobby Booth. He'd had a big row with Herbie and when his mam and dad didn't take his side he decided to run away. Herbie never got over that; I think he carried the guilt of it 'til the day he died. They found Bobby out there, on his back in the grass, unconscious. The rumour mill started grinding away, and word was he'd been found with nasty burns all over his face. Herbie told me the truth one day, walking home from school, how Bobby's wasn't burnt. Instead his head and shoulders were crumpled like old bedclothes.

"Like the oldest man you've ever seen," was how Herbie described his nine-year-old brother. "And the worst part is he doesn't know us?"

I asked him what he meant.

"He's like my grandad when he went full doolally at the end. Bobby just sits there in his chair, all wrinkled, and he dribbles food down his chin. He messes himself Jim, and my mam has to clean him up like a baby."

Herbie started to weep.

"The worst part is the few seconds when you think he *does* recognise you. His eyes goes wide and he looks confused, and panicked, and you're almost glad when he slips away again."

They shipped Bobby Booth off to a care home in Crowther. He died there when he was just thirty and as I've heard it told, when they did tests on his brain they found everything was desperately degenerated. Whether that's true or not I don't know, but I look at my fingers and feel the throbbing arthritis I've had in them for most of my life, and I wonder what would happen to a brain in that dark, clutching tunnel.

Gives me the shudders to consider it.

They put the damage done to Bobby down to a lightning strike, of all things. A bloody lightning strike on a clear, cold night and in the same field where Emily Lumb was last seen three years earlier. People 'round here might be small-minded and terminally incurious and wilfully-bloody-ignorant, but they aren't that stupid. Questions must have been asked in certain rooms, but none of it made it to the papers.

I had my own questions, though. First was why did Bobby not vanish like Emily and the rest? Funny that. It so happens that the night of Bobby's 'lightning strike' was the same weekend that Riot got out of our backyard. Unbeknownst to us, he'd spent most of the summer chewing on a one of the knackered fence posts at the bottom of the garden. We let him out for a pee on the Saturday night and when he didn't come back in, we found the splintered gap he'd made for himself.

I was bereft, and my dad wasn't much calmer, though he put a brave face on. Mam had only been gone a few months at that point, and it must have taken a lot for him not to dissolve. In many ways Riot had kept us afloat during the heaviest flood of grief. He'd shock a rare laugh out of us when one was most needed or fetch us one of his balls when we cried, 'cos he thought it would make us as happy as it made him. He was as much family as either of us.

"He'll be back, son." My dad didn't sound convinced.

All evening, we searched and paced and waited. I'd like to say it never occurred to me that he could have gone to the Square. That might be a lie that I told myself though. Was I so scared of that place that I was ready to let my friend face it alone?

I was sure he was dead. I even tried to reassure myself that he was with mam, curled up on settee made of cloud. It helped a little, but I still felt every ounce of his absence those two terrible nights.

Then, on the Monday morning, my dad had woken me up with a yell. I hadn't heard him that excited since before mam got poorly and I rushed downstairs, praying that it was Riot.

It was.

My dad had opened the front door for the milk and found him on the front step, fast asleep and filthy.

The three of us literally danced round the kitchen.

But when I got to school I heard about Bobby Booth. They'd found him late the night before.

I think Riot had known it was coming. Like a storm. I think the boggart had been gathering its strength, or its appetite, or whatever it does in the years after it takes someone, and I think Riot had sensed the threat pressure for a while, and because I refused to help him, he'd been working at that fence post in quiet determination. He'd got out and taken himself up there and he'd done his best to help poor Bobby, but he was either too late to stop the worst, or too small, 'cos he'd hardly grown an inch since he was a pup.

When I think about him working at that post, trotting up the lane alone and waiting for his fight, it makes me so proud of him. But anything could have happened: he could have been hit by a car, attacked by a bigger dog, or he could have frozen to death up there in the long grass, where I'm fairly sure he had spent the weekend.

That's when I knew I had to help.

I know I keep saying *this* got me moving, and *that* was the final straw, but I'll be honest: even with what had happened to Bobby Booth, I might still have deliberated longer, if it hadn't been for Lesley Anne Downey. That Christmas at the end of 1964, she was on every radio station and in every conversation across the garden fences. I can still picture her face from the missing posters. People like us, who were kids back then, we have those names and faces tattooed on the inside of our heads, don't we? Younger folk now, they have their own names, their own nightmares, but it's always the same story: an innocent child crosses paths with evil and they're never seen again.

Course, we found out that Brady and Hindley had taken her, and all the horrible things they'd done, the nightmares her mam had to hear on those tapes in the court. But for a while, as Christmas ticked over into New Year and the search for her went on and on, I wondered if she'd been snatched up by her own bog-gart. I felt terribly guilty. When I saw a photo of Lesley Ann's mam, looking frantically for some sign at that fairground in Ancoats, it made me think about Emily's mam, alone in her house up here, drinking herself silly. She had no more idea where her daughter was than Mrs Downey. Folk in Symester had taken to sneering at Barbara Lumb's dirty clothes and unwashed hair, but every time I saw her staggering home from the Bell and Kettle, I just felt sick.

After Bobby and Lesley Anne, I felt responsibility fall on me like the ceiling had given way. If I wasn't going to tell anyone what was going on up at the Square, then I had to do something about it myself, or there'd be more desperate mothers with never-answered questions. And, like I say, Riot was already eating his way through fences to do his part.

I went back to see George Cuddy, hoping for advice on what to do, but that time he kept me on his doorstep.

"I've got no answers, young Jim," he said. "You've got your dog and your young legs. I'm just a daft old fella who wants to be left alone." He shut his door against any further questions.

I stood there, winded with disappointment, and Riot seized his chance. He gave a tentative pull on his lead and I just thought, *ok then,* and let him tug me towards the bottom of Sheephead.

It was as simple as that. After years of avoiding even looking up this way if I could help it, I just gave in and followed my dog. Maybe it's 'cos I was old enough to shoulder it, or maybe it's just that you can only take so much looking away before you start to feel like things are your fault. What's that famous bit of the Bible? The one about putting down childish things? That's what I did that day on Mr Cuddy's front step. I put them down and I picked up what would be the rest of my life.

At first Riot was so delighted you'd think I'd given him all the tennis balls in the world. Have you ever seen a dog with a job? A sheepdog herding, a husky pulling? They have this swagger about them, and Riot was no different. No matter how short his legs were or how close his belly swung to the pavement, he let his mission carry him cheerfully all the way up the lane.

When he saw the boundary wall, though, his tail dropped, his ears flattened, and the fur around his neck stood up like a brush.

"It's ok, boy," I said, but he didn't need reassurance nearly as much as me. He wasn't scared, or not so I could tell, he was just solemn in a way I hadn't seen him since our very first meeting.

I'm not too proud to say he steadied my nerves, when all I wanted was to run all the way back down the lane. This patch of ground terrified me. It still does, if I'm honest, but it's a strange fear now, mostly buried under boredom. You do something as many times as I've walked 'round that field and it's impossible to keep the danger fresh in your mind. I reckon, that's why people who keep pet bears and tigers end up getting eaten.

I wasn't complacent that day though. No, that January evening I was fizzing with nerves. The fear was in me and around me. Even though the temperature was single digits, the air felt syrupy and cloying, like something nasty had pooled in the atmosphere. As we creaked open that gate my bad hand started tingling.

"Oh, boy. I'm not sure we should be doing this."

Riot turned his shaggy head with a look that said *well we're here now, so do it with me or let me go do it myself.*

It must sound daft, but I didn't want to disappoint him. I pushed down my own cowardice just enough to take a step through the gate. All the time I was scanning for any sign of the boggart, but the Square was just an empty stretch of land under a rusted metal sky. What are the chances that thing would come back at exactly the same hour of the same day that I'd returned, four years after our last encounter? People lived in these houses; there was no way the boggart was just wandering around this place willy-nilly. It'd have been spotted years ago.

Still, all the way around that first patrol, I felt watched.

We walked slowly. For the first time in his life Riot stopped pulling and fell into step beside me, or rather he set a pace and I matched it. The evening was coming in hard and I was deeply uneasy, but I knew we couldn't rush. Riot was in charge and I followed his lead. We travelled anticlockwise, starting at the gate. First we went down that long wall that divides the Square from the next field, then we traipsed along the edge of the long grass at the bottom, where I'd gone looking for my ball. It was only when we turned up the third side – along your garden fence – that I realised Riot was doing something peculiar. At each corner he'd stop, turnabout and pee. Then he'd scrabble at the ground to spread his scent in that way cocky terriers do. After setting off again he'd stop at the halfway point between the last corner and the next, and he'd repeat the ritual. There's nothing weird about a dog peeing, but it was so precise and measured. There was intent behind it.

If you stop and think, it makes sense. Dogs pee for a lot of reasons, but one of them is to give a warning, to say *this belongs to me, stay away.* And humans, we use salt circles and sage for protection, but witches and warlocks are known to combine urine into the mix for potency.

Riot wasn't just marking territory; he was casting a ward.

When we completed our perimeter tour at the gate, he peed one more time, shook himself, and gave me his usual daft grin. That was the Riot I knew. Not the strangely intense animal that'd just led me around the field.

It's turned out over the years that there are two Riots. The silly one, he belonged to me; the other one, he belonged only to himself, or maybe to some grander owner who we'll never know about, who lent him to us to keep this place safe.

Keep it safe he did. I don't know what went wrong the night that Bobby Booth was attacked, but this time it went right. As soon as we closed the circle with that last splash of dog pee, there was a slackening in the atmosphere. The twilight was still the colour of heavy steel, but the air felt less wet with dread. My fear was gone. I knew I could stand there all through the night and I'd be safe.

As if to prove the point, I took a tennis ball from my coat pocket where I always had one stashed. Riot went immediately manic, thrashing like a happy fish on a line. When I let him off his lead he pranced around, yipping for the ball like a banshee, as if he hadn't just put us through that whole stately ceremony.

We played a game of fetch, there in that field where I'd once nearly died a worse-than-death. We celebrated beating back the dark, just like we have for sixty-three years. The sun slipped away before we finished, but that was ok, 'cos night and darkness are two very different things.

"And you've done that every day since?" Margie asked.

"Aye. Give or take a few days here and there. Riot was desperate to go again the next day, and the next, so we just got into the habit."

"Did you have any help?"

"My dad filled in a few times. Once for a week when I was in bed with flu."

Margie thought about all the days of her life, stacked one atop the other. Every holiday, every impromptu trip away, and all the days that she'd felt down, ill or just plain lazy. She was awed by Jim's commitment to his duty, deluded or not.

"Did you ever tell your dad why?"

Jim shook his head.

"He was a good, kind bloke, but not one for nonsense. And this he'd have been sure to call nonsense."

"Then how did you get him to do what you needed?"

"I told him that Riot loved the Square, and my dad loved the dog to bits, so he was happy to oblige. After that, I just trusted Riot to do the rest."

"Did it work?" she asked. Against her better judgement, she was forgetting to lace her questions with doubt. Jim's story was seeping into her reality.

"Well, no more kids went missing," he replied. "But when I brought Riot up here after I'd been poorly that week, he was so frantic I thought he might have a seizure. We had to go around the Square half a dozen times 'til I was sure he couldn't have a drop left in him. Dad must have interrupted the ritual somehow. After that, I tended not to rely on anyone else."

"That's a lot of pressure when you're fifteen, Jim."

"It's a lot when you're fifty," he said. "But what could I do? Trouble is, you see, I've never known how often Riot has to make his circle. The longer we denied that thing a meal, the hungrier it would surely get. There's a chance I couldn't take a day off 'cos it'd strike at the first chance. With this new boy going missing when he did, seems I was right."

"So, you've been alone with this, all this time?"

"I think we're always alone with the things that really matter to us," he said.

Without any conscious decision to do so, Maggie reached across the table and laid her hand on top of Jim's. He twitched with surprise, and she wondered how long this man had gone without being touched. She didn't feel any attraction towards him, and she got no sense that he held any physical regard for her, but she felt him respond like a leaf to sunlight.

"Have you been happy, Jim?"

"Happy?" He said the word like he'd never considered it before. "What's that mean, really?"

"Staying here all these years. Doing this... job that you've set yourself. Has it been a good life?"

"It's been a useful life, I think. We kept the children safe."

Margie sighed. "Yes, you did. But has there been any joy?"

He took a moment to sip his drink and chew on the question. Slowly, a smile rose to his face. It was fragile and bittersweet but a smile, nonetheless.

"Aye, some."

I ran into Katherine Corder a week or so later. This was early 1965 and by then Riot and I had a routine of visiting the Square early in the morning or just before dark, when the place was generally empty. That day though, dad had got tickets for *Dr Terror's House of Horrors* at the Eureka, so I was taking care of business right after school. It's never seemed to make any difference what time we made the boundary. Though I've always been a bit nervous about doing early morning one day and waiting too long into the next.

It was one of those piercingly cold afternoons that come along in February to warn us that winter isn't done with the valley just yet. Every time Riot cocked his leg to make his mark, it steamed like a cauldron. The wind was a whip that had me swearing and Riot shivering through the woollen dog coat I'd bought him for Christmas. When we finally finished our circuit, I gave him a few extra biscuits and told him he was a tough lad.

"Your dog looks cold."

I spun round to find Katherine standing just outside the gate. With my cap pulled down over my ears, I hadn't heard her approach, and Riot hadn't given any sign either. That dog was only ever alert when it suited him. That day it suited him to let her get close.

"Hello, James."

"Hiya, Katherine."

I hadn't spoken to her in the two years since she'd left school. If two years was a big difference to children, then the chasm between a fifteen-year-old schoolboy and seventeen-year-old office girl was too wide to do anything but stare across. From time to time, I'd seen her through the window at Hawthorne's, the estate agents on Bridge Street. Terry Hawthorne was a sleazy bastard, even by standards back then, and I was surprised her mam and dad had let her take the job. But she'd put up with whatever hassle the old goat threw her way, and she looked every inch the grown up in her heels and red lipstick.

Yes, I may have spent quite a bit of time looking through Hawthorne's windows.

That day in the Square, Katherine didn't look so glamorous. A turned up coat collar couldn't keep the wind's wild grip out of her hair or the mascara from smearing her cheeks. She was still beautiful – she could never be anything less to me – but the weather had blown away the woman to reveal the girl.

"Are you coming in?" I asked, opening the gate for her.

"Thank you." She entered, rubbing her pale hands together. "It's so cold. Is your dog ok?"

"He's fine." I leaned down to scruff Riot's fur and he looked at me as if to say: *He's not fine. He'd like to go home please.*

"Poor thing. Couldn't you just let him stay by the fire?" She reached down to Riot, and gave him her fingers to lick, which he did with great relish.

"You're up here a lot, aren't you?" she asked.

I garbled an excuse about Riot liking to play in the Square. Though my reasoning must have looked fairly weak, considering the weather and how clearly Riot was *not* enjoying the experience. I felt absurdly guilty, as if I'd been caught doing something furtive.

Thankfully, Katherine's presence was just as odd. It was almost four in the afternoon and she should surely be at work. Plus, she was holding a bunch of flowers in one hand and a book in the other. As it was nearly Valentine's Day I thought she might be meeting someone up here. Though I couldn't have imagined a poorer setting for romance.

"These are for Emily," she said, as if reading my thoughts. "Today's the fourth anniversary."

"Oh... that's nice." I was aware that it was that time of year, but as so often in a young man's life, the details of other people's pain hadn't registered.

"I come every year and I bring her flowers and I think about her." Katherine's face sank. "Barbara used to join me here, but these days she doesn't even answer the door when I knock on."

We grimaced together, both picturing Barbara Lumb's life behind that door.

"Well, it's kind of you to do it for Emily."

"She was my best friend and a really nice person, and none of the things they say about her are true." Katherine's voice froze over. "I really hate this town."

Her anger surprised me. Despite spending every day helping ward off a monster, I was still happy enough in Symester. There's a comfort to being a young man in a place like this. You know every street, every snicket and ginnel; you know what you can get away with and what you can't, who you can talk back to, and who you really shouldn't. Those are the self-centred years of life, and you don't really see how people are being ground down around you. At that point I hadn't recognised Symester for what it could be: a sucking pit of a town, a bloody vacuum for hope.

Katherine was always ahead of me in that regard.

I still didn't know what to say next, so I stuttered out some nonsense and made for the gate. It was Katherine's book that stopped me. *Lady Chatterley's Lover*. I knew that creased, greasy orange cover very well. When it finally came out a few years earlier here, with all that row in the papers about it, Gordon Fox had managed to steal his brother's copy. We'd spent a hysterical afternoon reading out the racy parts and making daft noises. Though in truth I hadn't understood half of what the author was trying to say. It wasn't much of a story, if I remember right. I couldn't imagine why Katherine was carrying a copy around.

She must have noticed my attention. "Have you read this, James?"

I blushed.

"Bits of it."

"I bet." Her laughter was gentle, but my flush deepened.

"Emily and I were both reading it. Barbara had given Emily her copy, but I had to hide mine from my mam. I still do. 'Not under my roof young lady,' she'd say."

"Do you like it?" I asked, tentatively.

She nodded. "It's more romantic than dirty, but my mam wouldn't believe that. It just makes me sad that Emily never got to finish it, so every year I bring her some flowers and I read a few pages to her. By the time I'm an old lady we might have finished it."

Katherine thumbed through the book.

"There's this one line I can't stop thinking about. *A woman has to live her life, or to live to repent not having lived it.* There's something in that, don't you think?"

"Aye," I said. I'd been so preoccupied with watching her lips move, I hadn't listened to the words.

"Round here it feels like that's all any of us ever do. We repent not having lived." She palmed at a tear, spread the mascara in a crow's wing around her eye.

"Sorry, James. You must think I'm mad."

"No, not at all."

"Can I ask a favour?" she sounded nervous now. "Would you stay whilst I read to her?"

Despite the cold, I was so eager to say yes that my words jammed my mouth. Katherine mistook it as hesitation.

"It won't take long," she promised. "I'll just read a page or two and then we can go. It'd be nice not to walk back down on my own."

I assured her that I'd wait as long as she needed, and I glared at Riot, warning him not to make a fuss. To his credit, he just narrowed his eyes at the wind and settled in for my sake.

Katherine walked to the swing set. It was all rust and peeling lead paint, a scabby skeleton that threatened kids with lockjaw more than fun. But it was the last place that Katherine had been with Emily, so she tucked the flowers into the basket seat and began to read. I kept my distance and I couldn't hear which passages she chose, but for five minutes I watched a stream of emotions pour across her face. When she was finished she closed the book and palmed away another tear.

"I miss you, Em," she said. "Be well."

And with that Katherine's own ritual was over. Together we started back toward town, fogged in an awkwardness that neither of us had much clue how to lift. If not for Riot, those excruciating few minutes could have been the last time she and I ever spent together. Thankfully, there are two things that people can always talk about: the weather and dogs.

Katherine asked Riot's name and when I told her she laughed. A loud snort that in no way fit the way she looked. It was the first time I'd ever heard that particular laugh, and I loved it.

"Oh, that's a marvellous name." She bent down to fuss with him.

"Are you a riot, Riot? Are you a troublemaker?

Riot jumped up joyfully and planted a pair of muddy paws against Katherine's coat.

"Oh god, I'm sorry." I yanked him back on his lead.

"Don't be daft, James. We need some troublemakers round here. Don't we, Riot? Someone brave enough to misbehave." She reached for his lead. "Can I?"

I passed it to her with a warning that he would pull like mad. The little bugger proved me wrong, though.

He just strolled along happily at Katherine's feet, as if he knew how lucky he was and didn't want to spoil it.

By the time we reached the bottom of Sheephead, Katherine had fallen hard for my dog, and I'd fallen hard for her once more. We had to pass the top of my street to get to Whittaker Drive, where she lived in one of those big bungalows. She told me I should go home, that she'd be fine, but it was almost full dark and I told her my dad would be ashamed of me if he knew I hadn't escorted her home. That's the word I used: *escorted*. Like I was one of the soppy characters in her book. It's enough to make my toes curl even now. She seemed happy to be escorted though, and when we got to the turning for her road she made a big fuss of Riot, told me how nice it was to see me again. Then kissed me lightly on the cheek.

"Thanks for helping me remember her," she said.

I didn't reply. My mouth was dry as unbuttered toast.

"I'll see you around, James. Or is it Jim? That's what they call you, isn't it?

"James is fine," I said. I wanted to be James to her. A real name; a grown-up name. A *man's* name.

"Ok, James. Thanks for walking me home. You, too, Riot."

With that she left me there, a kite made of nerve endings, taking flight in the wind. The cold flared sharper where her lips had touched me and there wasn't a clear thought in my head.

Riot twitched his lead and we turned for home.

*

Three days later Katherine knocked on our door. My dad couldn't mask the surprise in his voice when he shouted up that I had a visitor. I pounded downstairs, expecting Gordon or one of the other lads, and stalled when I saw Katherine standing in our hallway. She wore the same black coat with the turned-up collar, a pair of charcoal cords and her hair was a chilly fall of liquid mahogany. As wintery as the outfit was, Katherine shone. There was never a time that she didn't make me want to stop and stare.

"Hello, James."

"Hiya!"

She smoothed her hair nervously and then beamed as Riot padded through from the kitchen to puncture the tension. After giving him his obligatory fuss, she asked if I'd like to go for a walk.

"A walk?" Honestly, all I remember from my first few meetings with Katherine was the feeling that something heavy was sitting on my tongue and, possibly, on my brain.

"Yes, a walk. You have a dog, so you walk, don't you?"

My dad was already fetching Riot's lead before I'd even had chance to agree that yes, I did indeed *walk.* As he handed it to me he slipped me a few shillings, using a sleight of hand I'd never suspected he possessed.

"It's cold out, Jim. Buy the lady a brew or something." He had a twinkle in his eye as he backed into the kitchen.

Katherine was busying herself with Riot, who was bouncing from paw to paw in excitement. That dog was delighted by any human being who wasn't the postman, but I'd rarely seen him as euphoric as when Katherine appeared. That never changed.

We walked for an hour that afternoon, until the wind cut into us so deeply that we took refuge inside Maggie Bentham's café. Maggie's been dead thirty years or more and her café is a Tesco Express now. But it was a warm hug of a place back then, and she let us bring Riot inside. I'm a sentimental old fool, but there are still times when I'm in there buying beans or a cut loaf, and I get a whiff of Maggie's home cooking and a trace of Katherine's Coty Wild Musk.

Katherine did most of the talking that first day. I found out that her mam had been diagnosed with breast cancer the year before, but there was hope she would get better. Worry showed on Katherine's face, though, and she gripped my hand when she said how sorry she was for my loss. Later I'd feel terribly guilty that the touch of her fingers could momentarily wipe my grief clean, but I suspect mam would've just been happy that I was happy. And I was. God I was. I listened whilst Katherine told me about her plans to go to some art school in London if she could save enough money, and that took us to her job and Terry Hawthorne. He was indeed a nightmare, she admitted. All sneaky hands and off-colour comments. Katherine could laugh about it, but it made me want to pull the bloke's head off the top of his neck.

"Him and my dad are friends," she said, when I asked her if she'd told her parents. "But don't worry. I can handle Terry. He's all belly and no bollocks."

I must've looked shocked, 'cos she snorted. "What? Do you think I'm all sweetness and light, James? Far from it."

She was sweetness and the brightest of lights, but she had a mouth like a lorry driver, too. That piglet laugh of hers, when she was caught off guard. I still laugh myself just thinking about it.

After that I was sunk. Katherine called for me again a week later, then a few days after that, and then it was two days in a row and soon I was walking Riot around to her house and returning the favour. Naturally, I wondered why she wanted to spend time with me, but I reminded myself her mam was ill. Katherine probably appreciated my understanding of the situation, I thought.

Plus, she loved my dog. She never got tired of Riot. When even I got sick to the back teeth of telling him how he had to drop the ball if he wanted me to throw it, she'd just wait patiently until he relinquished it, then she'd chuck it for him and begin the whole process again.

"He really loves you," I said one day that summer. *And I do, too* was hidden in that, but perhaps not as deep as I would've liked, 'cos she kept my eye a little too long.

"He's wonderful," she said. "I'm so glad I met him."

There wasn't much to say to that, so I held my nerve and held her gaze and held my tongue.

Finally, as a soggy May gave way to the hope of summer, she confronted me.

"Why are you so obsessed with the Square, James?"

I spluttered some protest; told her that Riot just liked to chase his ball there.

"James, that dog would happily chase a ball down the white line of Bridge Street if you threw it for him. There's got to be some other reason you take him up there *every single day*. And I just don't get it. It's such a nasty place."

"I don't know what you mean, Kath." Lying has never come natural to me. For most people that would be a good thing, wouldn't it? But for me, with my life, a bad poker face has always been a weakness.

"Tell me something." Katherine dropped her voice. We were sitting on the benches out front of St Michael's, eating chips from the paper, and she didn't want anyone to hear us.

"Have you ever seen anything odd up there?"

"Odd?" I tried to summon a laugh, but it caught in my throat.

"Anything that frightened you?" She searched my face. "I've heard rumours."

"What kind of rumours?"

"You know, the stories some old people tell around here. The boggart."

It was the first time I'd ever heard anyone other than George Cuddy say that word out loud. Something clearly showed in my reaction 'cos Katherine pressed on.

"That's where it's supposed to live, isn't it? Up there, where Emily was taken?"

She'd been doing her research, too, it seemed.

"I don't know what you mean?" I said, weakly.

"Barbara told me she saw something once. Back when Emily first went missing, her mam was out every night with a torch, hoping she'd find her, or at least some trace. One night, she says, she was leaving, when she saw someone standing by the gate. Skinny bloke, that's how she described him, scruffy and old-fashioned with a horrible smile. A piranha smile she called it. Barbara says she shouted out to him, but by the time she got to the gate, he'd gone."

My hands were clenched around the bag of chips.

"Course," Katherine continued, "when she told the police they didn't do a thing, and that's when Barbara started drinking. She told me that's when she knew she wasn't going to get Emily back."

It was a mild evening, but I felt a chill spread through my guts. The thought of meeting that thing in the night, its leering face catching you off guard. For a second I was back there, on the edge of my own vanishing.

I shuddered, and Katherine raised an eyebrow.

"And there's you," she said, "going up there every day, rain or shine, to walk around an ugly patch of grass when there's a decent park just behind this church. Seems a funny thing to me."

I almost told her, I really did, 'cos part of me thought she might believe me. A terrible, haunted part of me still thinks we could have been partners in this. But just like my parents, the thought of her worst reaction to my lunatic story was too great a risk to take. Instead, I said that I felt sorry for Barbara and I understood why she'd clutch at local tales, but that had nothing to do with me.

"Riot really does just like it," I insisted. "You should see how he pulls to get up there."

"You're not telling me something, James." She searched my face.

There's so much I'm not telling you, I thought. *A long list that starts with a monster and ends with I love you.*

"It's a creepy place at night," I agreed. "I'm not surprised that Barbara got scared."

"Do you not get scared up there, James?"

"Me?" I made a pshewing sound and flexed my skinny arms. "No, 'cos I've got Riot and together we're brave."

A degree of humour had crept back into Katherine's face, along with some mischief.

"How brave are you, exactly?" She glanced at the empty street and leaned closer to me on the bench.

"Erm..." I was suddenly lost for words, thought and breath.

"Be brave, James," she whispered.

I'd survived a monster and spent half the year fending it off but, right then, I was more scared than I'd ever been. Time turned to honey and I had the clear space to think, *oh please let her mean this* and then I was kissing her. Kissing Katherine Corder on a summer evening as the sun bathed us both in its goodnight warmth. If the grip of those tendrils inside the boggart was the worse sensation of my life, that was the best. There was a weight to her kiss, her mouth pressed against mine with urgency and substance and intent. It felt like a battle as much as a blessing.

Finally, after an age and a single heartbeat, she pulled away.

"Well, it's about time we did that, don't you think?" She grinned. "Come on, let's go get Riot and tell him the good news."

With that, she was up and moving. I just followed.

It was a long time until I stopped following Katherine. Finally, of course, she went where I couldn't accompany her, but right until the end of our time together, she led the way.

There's no need to recount the details of a young love affair, 'cos young love is boring for anyone who isn't part of it. If young love lasts long enough to become adult love and then old love, that's when it gets interesting again. Katherine and I just made the first stage, but we missed the rest.

We were together for six years. No one expected that, least of all me. For months I clung on to what was growing between us like it was a bike with no brakes. In those days it was normal for an older lad to have a younger girlfriend, but not vice versa. Yet if she was ever embarrassed to be seen with me, she didn't show it.

I left school without taking my O-levels 'cos I so badly wanted to get a job and be a man with a wage and a girl to spend it on. God, the things we thought manhood meant back then! My dad was furious. He shouted at me for weeks about how I was "throwing my life away for a girl". Dad loved Katherine to bits, but he cooled on us being together after that. I'm glad he lived long enough to see me study to be a teacher, 'cos he was right all along, but at sixteen you don't ever believe anyone is right except yourself.

They took me on as an apprentice at Cromwells, the shoe factory on Manchester Road. It was furiously hot in summer, frigid in winter, and they worked piece-work, so if you got in the way you were costing people their bonus, and you got put in your place quickly, and sometimes, violently. After a year I progressed to the line, where I spent my days pinning soles or gluing uppers. I still shiver at the thought of those shifts, counting the grains of my life in hours and left feet.

I saw Katherine nearly every day. She lived with her parents and I stayed with my dad, and we would sneak around trying to find time alone together. We first made love when I'd just turned sixteen, whilst dad made himself scarce at a darts tournament.

"Be careful, son," he said to me sternly, before leaving for the night.

I won't say anything about that evening other than it was frightening and full of wonder.

When one year together turned to three, and then five, Katherine's parents started making life difficult. Ours was supposed to be a puppy love that would fade within the year, not toughen and endure. They wanted better for their little girl than a line-worker in a shoe factory. Can't say they were wrong on that score, but it made Katherine so angry. I used to talk her down.

Her mam, Gwen, was a nice enough lady, made small and nervous by her close call with cancer, and by her husband. Kenneth Corder was the kind of bloke who typifies this town for me. A golf club bully, full up with his own opinions on the world, no matter how little of it he'd seen beyond his telly and papers. He thought owning a Volvo was ultimate mark of a man, and I'm not sure what made him dislike me more: his daughter's affection for me or how unimpressed I was by his standing in town. Once, over dinner, I made some small comment in defence of those women who went on strike at the Ford plant down south. Kenneth called me a dirty Leninist bastard and left the table.

He also hated Riot and wouldn't ever let him in the house. That annoyed me more than anything, but it was an excuse to avoid the place.

Katherine loved her parents, but she found them wearying. They were a big part of her desperation to escape the valley, though they'd be horrified to hear her talk about art schools in London or Glasgow, how we could go together and I could find work whilst she studied. We'd spend hours lying on my bed, whilst she leafed through art books, dwelling on the paintings that inspired her most. Katherine would point out all the secrets that unlocked their meaning, but towards the end of us, I saw those brushstrokes as cage bars with her on one side and me here, painted in amongst these hills.

Because I still had Riot and our watch, didn't I? Neither love nor split shifts got in my way, though they made it trickier. Often, I'd find myself arriving at the Square with the dawn or leaving with the last gasp of sunset at my back.

It worked though. Nobody else went missing, there were no repeats of what had happened to poor Bobby Booth, and over the first five years of my courtship with Katherine, the motivation to keep dragging myself up there did begin to wane. More and more, I'd find myself considering whether we'd done our job and scared that thing away for good. On really rainy days, or on those stolen afternoons when the last thing I wanted was to drag myself away from Katherine's dozing body, I'd look at my hand and force the memory of that terror. Over time even that started to lose its power. As I approached my twentieth birthday, it was really Riot that kept us going. Every day, without fail, he'd take himself to the front door and convince me to do once more what *he* still thought necessary.

I've mentioned so many forks in the road, haven't I? What would have happened if I hadn't been at the Square that day when I was eleven, if I hadn't overheard George and my dad talking, and if George hadn't answered his door when I knocked? What about if my mam had stuck to her guns about giving Riot away? Who knows? Well, if my dad hadn't had his heart attack in October of 1969, I might have left Symester that year. My staying wasn't for the reasons you'd expect, either. I didn't stick around to nurse my old man in his dotage. He was only in his early fifties when he collapsed at the bar of the Bell and Kettle, and he made a fine recovery. He lived 'til he was my age now, and he never needed much help up until the day he died.

No, my dad's trip to the hospital kept me here 'cos it showed me once and for all how important mine and Riot's job was, and how thin the tightrope we had to walk to do it.

The whole nightmare started with a hammering on our front door on a Friday afternoon. I'd finished an early shift and I was half-asleep on the sofa, with a Gary Cooper western on the telly. My treacly brain confused the knocking with the cowboys' guns. When I finally opened the door, the man on the other side nearly fell into our house. It was John Leede, a drinking and darts mate of my dad's, who also worked with me at Cromwells.

"It's your dad, Jim. He's had a bad turn."

He said more, but everything after the words *his heart* was just white noise. Whilst John wittered from the front step, I frantically collected my wallet and keys and called Riot back to the front room. I should have noticed how unsettled he seemed, but my mind was rushing elsewhere.

"You wait here, boy. I'll get someone to come and look after you." I had no idea who. Katherine would want to be with me and, though I could ask her parents, I doubted they'd be willing to take my dog in for the night.

"Hurry up, Jim. I'll run you up to the hospital myself."

There was nothing I could do except stroke Riot and tell him I'd be back as soon as I could. He whined as I closed him in the front room, but John practically tugged me out of the house and pointed me to the passenger seat of a chocolate brown Austin 1100.

On the way to the hospital, he told me that my dad had just keeled over at the bar and that the young barmaid had done chest compressions until the ambulance arrived. They'd rushed him to Crowther General.

"If he lives, he'll have a lot to thank Fiona for," John said, then paled at his own word choice.

If.

I was at the hospital for a few hours alone until Katherine arrived with her parents. They sat stiff and mostly silent whilst she held me and told me that it was ok if I needed to cry. I've never been one for crying though, not after mam died. That reservoir has never refilled properly.

The four of us sat for another hour or two, nursing appalling cups of tea and trying to avoid the fact that my dad was struggling to live just a corridor away. Katherine's mam made a few efforts at conversation, but Kenneth just sat ramrod straight in his chair, endlessly flicking the nails of his thumb and finger together. After a while, I wanted to murder him just to make the sound stop.

"You three should get off home," I said. "It's late and there's nothing you can do here."

Katherine immediately protested, but Kenneth seized on the opportunity.

"The lad's right, Kath. There's nothing you can do. And you've got work tomorrow."

"Never mind work," she said, appalled. "Terry can piss off."

Kenneth turned puce at that. He looked like an infuriated sea lion, with his bald head and a coarse moustache. Normally I enjoyed seeing him boil over, but right then, I just wanted him gone.

"No, please," I chipped in. "I need you to check on Riot."

When I said his name, my stomach fell to my feet.

We hadn't been to the Square yet that day.

A generous soul might say that I had good reason to forget, but I'd spent almost five years of my life circling that damn field, it was as natural as brushing my teeth in the morning or checking the doors at night. Even worse, the drive to Crowther had taken us up Sheephead, *past* the Square, yet my brain hadn't even registered it. Riot knew, of course. He'd already been restless when I left the house. I pictured him at home, growing anxious, then frantic, confused about where I was and why we weren't doing what we were supposed to.

If I truly came close to crying that night, it was then, from frustration.

Katherine was almost in tears herself. "But you can't stay here on your own, James. Why don't you stay at ours for the night. We can pick Riot up on the way."

Kenneth started at that. "Oh, I don't think we—"

"Dad," she snapped. "Don't be so cruel. We'll take him."

Her dad wilted, but he shot me a resentful glare.

I hugged Katherine. "Go, Kath. Look after Riot. He'll be missing me and glad to see you. But listen," I dropped my voice, "I can't explain why right now, but there's a thing I need you to do..."

She tried to pull away when I mentioned the Square, but I held her close and whispered the rules of the warding. I didn't call it that, of course. I just said that Riot would know what to do if she let him, though, no doubt that sounded just as mad.

When we separated her wide eyes were full of hurt, at the half-truth when I'd lied to her for so long.

"I know it's late, so ask your dad to go up there with you. But please do this for me, Kath. Will you?"

She nodded. "But then we need to talk."

With severe reluctance, she followed her parents out of the hospital, leaving me alone with my dread and a two-day old copy of *The Mirror*.

I already told you that my dad pulled through, but for all of that long, terrifying night and a chunk of the next day, he hovered on the cusp. I had a sickening conversation just before midnight, with a doctor who told me that I should prepare for the worse. As if that were possible. The worst is always something you haven't thought of yet.

The nurses told me that I could go home and they'd ring me if anything happened, but with no car and no one to call at that hour, I couldn't leave. And what if I did get a lift home and they called to say my dad was going, how would I get back in time? I couldn't trust Kenneth to drive me, and back then there was only one taxi in Symester, manned by a happy drunk called Derry Johnson, who turned up to bookings if he was in the right mood and the pubs were shut.

I told the staff I wasn't going anywhere and in the early hours a young Indian nurse took pity and made me up a rough bed across three chairs in an empty storeroom. Deepa, she was called. I'll never forget that 'cos she did me such a great kindness, but I've never suffered a longer or more uncomfortable night.

Early the following afternoon, I was told that my dad was out of surgery and conscious. He'd been very lucky, the doc said, and there would be a long recovery ahead, but I could see him if I liked. I rushed down the hallway to his room, only to find a husk of my father staring up at me from the bed.

"Hiya, son," he croaked.

I couldn't hug him, but I clutched his hand until he winced.

"Ease up, Jim, else you'll put me in the bloody hospital." His laugh was pained.

We talked for a while until the nurses finally decided to kick me out.

"Will you go home *now*, lad?" an older nurse asked. "Dutiful son is one thing, but we might have to start charging you rent."

"What?" my dad asked. "He hasn't been home?"

"No, Mr Howarth. He's been sitting out there all night worrying about you."

"Daft bugger." He relinquished my hand. "Go. Riot must be dying for a walk."

I kissed his yellowed cheek, told him I'd be back that evening, and asked the nurse if there was a phone I could use. She sent me to the front desk.

It was Gwen who answered the phone.

"Corder residence," she trilled. "Oh, hello, James. How's your dad?"

I told her what the doctors has said and she sounded genuinely pleased for me. In the background of the call, I heard approaching thunder.

"Katherine's not here," she replied to my request. "She had to go to work. Shall I get her to—"

There was a loud scratching noise down the line and suddenly Kenneth was barking at me.

"What do you think you're playing at, asking my daughter to take your scraggy mutt up the back of beyond in the middle of the night? Shame on you, boy. Do you think it's right to have her up there where that girl went missing?"

The "boy" rankled me, but my stomach turned over with bigger concerns.

"Please tell me she took him," I said.

"She bloody well did *not*. You're lucky we even took the dog in at all, the stink and noise of the bleedin' thing."

I felt sick.

In the background Gwen was remonstrating with him, but Kenneth shushed her and droned on. "All damn night at the door, wailing its bleedin' head off. I work hard and I need my sleep. Our Kath needs her sleep, too, and you expect us to stay up all night with a mongrel you've not trained properly. Not on your life, boy. If our Kath didn't have such a kind heart that mutt would've been out of here a lot earlier than it was."

"What do you mean," I cried "Where is he?"

"Back where he bloody belongs, at your house. I tied him up outside. I hope someone's nicked him, though. I don't know why anyone would want the nasty little shite. Just like I don't know why our Kath would want you."

The slamming phone cracked against my eardrum.

Panic chased me all the way back to Symester. It took me ten minutes to find the bus stop going my way and, of course, I'd just missed one so had to wait forty minutes for the next. Crowther General was only five miles from home and I gave serious thought to walking or trying to thumb a lift, but the bus seemed the less risky option. When it finally arrived, ten minutes late, I was so rude to the driver he nearly kicked me off. I backed down and begged until he gave me a ticket and told me to sit down and "shut my hole".

It was Saturday afternoon, which meant two things: One, there were likely to be kids playing in the Square, and two, this was easily the longest Riot and I had gone without making our rounds. We last went up after my shift on Thursday.

As the bus rolled down Sheephead, I saw children in the Square. A group of four. None of them looked older than ten, and one little girl could have been as young as six. They were running around playing some kind of tag, cheerful and oblivious to the dwindling day. My watch said it was half past four; beyond the Square the sun was already beginning its sharp descent to kiss the hills.

"Come on," I hissed, urging the bus to go faster. What would happen if I got off alone, I wondered? Would I be able to do anything without Riot? I doubted it. It had been him, or some version of him that had deterred the boggart all these years, at least if George's tale and his collected documents were to be trusted. Right then I did trust them. All the months of my slowly weakening resolve felt like a soft dream. As the Square and the children fell out of sight behind us, I believed absolutely in the danger that place posed.

The bus dropped me a few streets from home. In my panic about the Square, I hadn't given much thought to Riot himself, but Kenneth's words hit me afresh.

How long had the poor dog been tied up outside. It was chilly. Did he have water?

What if someone had taken him?

The moment I turned the corner of our street, Riot's wild barking told me that at least he was still there.

When I came through the gate he nearly broke his neck trying to reach me. He was tied to the downspout by a rough length of rope, and I was horrified to see that a good length of it was stained crimson. The same colour coated Riot's mouth. He'd tried to chew his way through the rope, and cut his gums open in the process. He'd pulled so hard at the downspout he'd half-torn the bracket from the masonry.

"Oh god, boy. I'm sorry." I decided right then that Kenneth Corder was going to have some very bad luck in the very near future.

"I know, I know." I stroked Riot vigorously with my clumsy hand, whilst I untied the rope from the spout with the other. There wasn't even time to go inside and get his collar. We needed to go *now*.

The moment I released him Riot pulled for the gate. I held onto the rope as best I could as he dragged me all the way to the bottom of Sheephead. We started that long climb at pace, but Riot was already half-exhausted and his short legs could only carry him so fast. Halfway up the hill he was panting, and his tongue hung heavily from the side of his mouth.

"Calm down, lad. Save your energy." I didn't dare think what he might need it for.

My anxiety started to abate as we drew closer to the Square. There was still light in the sky and, though the children had been very young, they were together. Surely the boggart couldn't tackle four of them at once, I thought. When we got there, we'd freshen the ward and find some way to encourage the kids to get back down to town.

"It'll be fine, mate," I said, but as the words left my mouth, Riot started pulling again. When I looked up I realised why, and I felt the world turn cold.

Walking towards us were two of the four children. One girl, one boy. Neither of them was the six-year-old. As we came together the girl cooed at Riot, but we didn't have time for that.

"Where are your friends?" I barked.

They both cringed away.

"Sorry, didn't mean to shout. But shouldn't you kids stick together? It's going dark."

The boy still looked dubious. Quite rightly, I suppose. The Moors Murders weren't that long ago and mothers still warned their kids about strange men. I certainly must've seemed strange. After all, who was I and what did I know about his friends?

The girl was less on her guard.

"They're up at the Square," she said. "Gary knocked Bethany over, and Johnny threatened to batter him. So, we left, 'cos our Gary's scared."

"Shurrup," the boy snapped. "I never meant to knock her over. And I'm *not* scared."

He marched past us.

"He *is* so scared," the girl said with a smirk. Then she followed her brother.

The sky was purpling in earnest. The trees that overhung that last stretch of the lane before the Square, cast shadows like arms, reaching for me and Riot, as if to trip us. When the gate at last hove into view, Riot began to whine.

It was swinging in the breeze.

Please be gone, please be gone, I thought, then realised what *gone* could mean. As we drew level with the gate, Riot's nervous griping became a full-throated growl.

"Oh god," I said, out loud.

There was a man in the field with his back to me.

I recognised the grey clothing.

The felt cap.

The thin limbs.

"Get away, kids," I yelled, but they didn't look away from the figure approaching them. I remembered that paralysis, and even though I couldn't see the grin on that dreadful face, I knew how wrong it looked, how off kilter with the world. And though the boy ignored my cry, he stepped in front of the little girl with a timid bravery that hurt my heart.

The boggart ignored me, too. But he couldn't ignore Riot.

When I let go of the rope Riot moved faster than I'd ever seen him move. It was as if all the years of throwing tennis balls had been preparation for this single life-or-death, all-or-nothing sprint into war. He skimmed the grass like a stone across a still lake, like silk across skin.

He was beautiful.

The boggart turned just as Riot made his leap. There was still a trace of that oversized smile on his face, but it dropped away as my dog barrelled into him, snarling and snapping. Last time Riot had been too small to do any damage; this time he was grown and eager to hurt. He must have sunk his teeth somewhere because the boggart screamed.

"Come here," I gestured wildly to the kids, and they broke toward me, the boy herding the girl in front of him. I pushed them behind me, but kept my eyes on my dog, who was literally clawing his way up the boggart's body, aiming for his neck. Only a corduroy covered forearm was keeping him at bay.

Riot was fearless, but I watched with horror as the boggart pulled at the buttons of his overalls. I knew well what was under there and Riot was pressed against the boggart's midsection, separated only from the pit by a thin layer of cotton.

"Down, Riot," I commanded. But he was beyond that. A red curtain had descended.

The boggart ripped at the buttons and several of them gave way. The overalls fell partly open and something shifted in the boggart's posture. Suddenly, rather than trying to push Riot away, he began to pull him inwards, towards the waiting cavity. Just like he had with me.

Riot's claws scrabbled for purchase against flesh that wasn't there.

"Wait here... or run," I said to the kids. It's awful to say but, right then, I only cared about my dog. I ran to save him.

Riot squealed as part of him was fed to the darkness, but still, he wouldn't stop trying to savage the enemy. With a big lunge he managed to snap his teeth closed around the boggart's jaw, and then they were both crying out in pain. I saw the boggart raise his arms for one big shove that would dislodge the teeth and send Riot falling into that hole.

But then I was there. Already swinging.

"Put him DOWN," I yelled, and I threw the hardest punch I could. I'd never hit anyone before, and never since, but I tell you, that one would do for a lifetime.

The boggarts eye's rolled white and he staggered backwards. Riot dropped to the ground and tried to continue the fight, but he was done. His tail and most of his hindquarters were stripped down to the skin in raw tiger stripes. Beads of blood popped to the surface in the hairless channels. It looked like he'd been whipped and burned. I didn't know if he was dying.

Still, he crawled towards the boggart, who was backing away groggily. Supernatural demon or not, it seemed he was as susceptible to a smack in the face as any of us.

Perhaps I should have helped Riot finish the job. Could I have held him down whilst Riot ripped at his throat. Maybe that would have ended all of this for good. Or it could have ended Riot, who was now lying on his side and panting in pain. I had no idea what that thing was capable of, even as weakened as it seemed to be.

I picked my dog up, trying to be gentle with his wounds, but still he whimpered. I cursed myself, 'cos if I hadn't missed our patrol, this fight would never have been needed.

"Never again, boy," I promised. "I won't make a mistake again."

The boggart was almost to the gate.

He spat malice at us in a language I've never heard before or since. I'm not even sure they were words, but the message was clear and hateful.

"Get gone," I shouted. "And stay gone. Next time we'll kill you."

My words sounded as hollow as the body inside his grey clothes, but he minded me. In the time it took me to check for the children, I heard a sharp pop and he was gone. So were the kids, though not with him. Good for them. I wondered what they would tell their parents.

Riot mewled in my arms. His blood had slicked my hands and, though I tried my best not to touch the raw stripes in his flesh, they crisscrossed his rump so closely that it was impossible to avoid them. Despite the pain of the burns, Riot's eyes were clear. I kissed his nose, not caring about the blood that speckled his muzzle.

"We won, boy," I said. "We won again."

His tail beat a lethargic rhythm against my arm.

We won. Just. But at what cost?

The clock told Margie that this time Jim had been speaking for a solid hour without interruption. He'd been in her kitchen since just before six and now it was approaching nine at night. She couldn't recall the last time she'd had a conversation of this depth or intimacy, certainly the last was long before Don died. In truth, had they ever talked like this, even in the early, incendiary days of their marriage? She didn't think so.

Now, Jim slumped. He looked spent and empty, but he couldn't stop now. Margie had to know more.

"What happened to Riot?"

"He healed."

"What? All of that damage, and he just got better?"

Jim dragged himself upright in the chair. "Aye. I carried him home, just like on that first day, and I bathed him softly as I could. He cried and went all whale-eyed and it nearly made me scream to hurt him, but I salved his wounds with jelly and eventually he fell asleep in my lap. It was a hard night."

Margie poured them both another tot of whisky. She saw with some alarm that more than half the bottle had gone, and much of it into her. A headache beckoned in the morning.

Now that she'd got Jim going again, he wasn't stopping. "I had to call the hospital to tell them that I wouldn't be back that evening. Nurse Deepa was back on shift and she said my dad was doing well, that there was no great reason to worry, and I should get my rest."

"Deepa?" Margie interrupted. "Short woman, soft voice?"

"That sounds like her, aye."

"Bloody hell!" Margie marvelled. "Deepa Vishwakarma. I worked with her at Crowther when I was a trainee. She was formidable."

"But very kind," Jim insisted. "And she was young then and keen to help. I asked her how to treat burns, told her I'd grabbed hold of a hot pan and blistered my hand badly. I think her advice was a big part of why Riot got better so soon."

"How soon?"

"Within a week the skin was healed. Dry and scaly but not raw. His fur took a lot longer to grow back in, and it was always coarser along those lines. But do you know the most amazing thing?"

Margie could guess, but she let him continue.

"The next morning, I woke up on the settee and Riot wasn't by my side. He was by the back door, ready to go back up to the Square."

"Did you take him?"

"Yes. I didn't want to, but it wasn't fair to Riot to let his pain go to waste by just giving that thing an open goal. There was no way he could walk it on his own, so I carried him up there, helped him limp around the field, and then carried him all the way home again. I worried how we'd cope going forward, but he got better so quickly. I've never known whether it was because he was magic, or just because he was just so tough."

All evening Jim had talked about Riot with a calm voice and a neutral face. Now, he craned his neck and gave the bag a look of such love and grief that Margie felt tears crowd the back of her eyes.

Margie wanted to rescue him from sadness so she pivoted to anger.

"What happened with Katherine and her dad? He sounds a right piece of work."

"Oh, Kenneth?" Jim fashioned a nasty smile. "I punished him the best way I knew how. I killed the thing he loved best."

Margie flinched.

"Relax, Margie. I mean his car. That Volvo Amazon he was so proud of. I followed him to the Conservative Club the next Saturday night. They were having a party and the music was good camouflage."

"What did you do?"

"I smashed it. Every panel, every window. The wing mirrors, the bonnet. I went at that car like a devil, and every time I swung that lump hammer, I pictured Riot's mouth, all bloodied up from chewing on that rope. But deep down, I think I was swinging at this town. At all the nasty, small-minded bastards who were still around, dancing inside that Club, when my mam was gone, and Emily Lumb was gone, and Billy Booth was gone. I've never been a violent man, but I hate to think what would've happened if Kenneth had come outside and seen me with that hammer."

He sucked in a breath and his smile softened at the corners.

"You've come all this way with me, Margie. Don't go thinking I'm crazy now. I was a young man, and angry. It bloody-well worked, too. Katherine told me her dad cried his eyes out when he saw the damage."

Margie had to admit she enjoyed the justice. She'd gotten so sucked into Jim's tale that she hated Kenneth, this man she never met, who once mistreated a dog that she surely couldn't believe in. Yet, she did believe. She wouldn't ever say it out loud outside this kitchen, outside her own head, but she believed Jim's story.

So, with that in mind, she thought, good riddance to Kenneth Corder and his Volvo Amazon.

"Did Katherine know it was you who did it?"

"I think she suspected," Jim said.

"And what happened with you two?"

He sighed. "That's a sadder story."

Katherine was upset that I'd lied to her about the Square. She kept her anger in check for the first few days, whilst dad got over the worst, but it was obvious there was a strain between us. With dad in hospital, for the first time in our lives we had a house entirely to ourselves. Yet, Katherine paid me only short and strangely polite visits. She never once asked what Riot and I had been up to, nor did she question the lie that Riot's stripped fur was caused by him getting caught in barbed wire. That entire autumn and early winter was a period of uneasy quiet, with neither of us saying out loud any of the things that we thought about every time we met.

It came to a head on New Year's Eve. My dad was home by then but still only a pale wax moulding of himself. He took himself off to bed well before midnight, leaving Katherine sitting on the settee, absently watching Lulu sing in the new year. I reached for Katherine's hand and that's when she said she was leaving.

For a slow second I thought she meant she was going home for the night. Then I saw the quiver in her lip and I understood.

She'd gotten a placement at an art college in London. Her parents were furious, but Katherine was determined to go. She'd saved the best part of three years' wages and, though her course wouldn't start until the summer, she planned to move early in the new year and find a short-term job and somewhere to live. Terry Hawthorne was starting to get more persistent with his slippery hands, and she couldn't stand to work for him anymore.

"I need to go, James. I need to get out."

"Ok," I said.

"You could come with me."

She spoke kindly but with resignation. She already knew I wouldn't be going with her. I'm just not sure, deep down, how bereft or relieved she was about that. Don't get me wrong, Katherine loved me. I'd come to believe that, truly. But I had the stink of this valley about me in a way that she didn't. I would be the Symester soil stuck in her boots, the quarry grit in her hair, the smell of farming in her clothes: all things that she would carry with her for a time but soon wash away in her new, clean life.

"Kath…" I stammered something about my dad needing me, and she waited for me to finish before calling me out.

"Is that really why you're staying, James? For your dad? Or is it for the crusade you and that dog of yours are on, up there, in that field?"

For the millionth time in the presence of Katherine Corder, I had no idea what to say.

"Whatever it is your doing, whatever you think you're achieving, I hope it's worth your life, my love." Her tears spilled over. Not being the crying type, I just sat dumb, but I was reeling around inside.

"Because that's what you're giving," she said. "Your life. To this place."

I wanted to tell her about the boggart. Right then I *knew* she would have believed me. She might have stayed, she might have helped me, and that would have been beautiful for a month, maybe a year. Then the bitterness would rise like dirty water, and we'd drown in it. She called it a crusade, but really it's a cage. My cage. Mine and Riot's alone. There couldn't be any justification for locking Katherine in with us.

"I'm sorry," is all I could say.

"I know you are, James. I hope you won't be forever."

We talked for a while longer, but soon she said she had to go. She kissed me fiercely, that same bullying kiss that she always pressed upon me, as if love was a competition.

"I'll miss you," she said.

Riot lifted his head from his bed and watched us with wary eyes. He knew something was wrong.

"I'll miss you, too, Riot." She ruffled his fur with false merriness. "You and your dad here will have to come down on the train to see me."

"We will, wont we, boy?" It was another lie, but the kindest one I could summon.

"Look after him, Riot," she said, and kissed his white patch. "Look after each other."

Then she was at the door, and it was all happening with such dizzying speed. Remember I started this story saying it's hard to recognise life-changing moments? Well, I grasped Katherine's departure from my life with excruciating clarity.

She got a few steps down the path and turned. In the moonlight, her hair was threaded with quartz.

"Remember what that book said, James. *You have to live your life, or live to repent not having lived it.*"

And then she was gone.

I went back inside on jelly legs. Riot met me at the door, head cocked in confusion, whilst he peered outside for Katherine. When he couldn't see her he let out a long, low whine. It sounded like goodbye.

"I know, boy. I know. But you've still got me."

Together we flopped on the settee and Riot stretched up to lick my face, then placed his head on my thigh. On the telly, the band were singing Auld Lang Syne. We were in a whole a new decade.

"You let her go," Margie said. She felt a depth of sorrow for Jim. He had a stoic face, but the last few hours had given her a crash course in tracing the emotion he barred behind his wrinkles. There was a tightness to his jaw that suggested he could still bite down on this pain like a sore tooth, half a century later.

"I had to," he said, simply. "I couldn't steal her life."

"Would it have been so bad for her, staying here?" Margie felt a little resentful of the idea that the life she had made for herself in Symester could be so urgently considered something to escape.

"For her, it would've been. Aye."

Margie let it go.

"What became of her?" she asked.

"She made her art. That's all I know and that's all I really care about. She didn't come back often, but when she did, we would say hello like we were just what we were: people we used to know. She'd always point out that Riot didn't look a day older and I made a joke of it every time, until it got so it wasn't funny anymore."

"After a while she stopped coming back altogether. She stayed down south and painted beautiful things. I have a print of one at home. I'd love to buy an original, but you know what art like that costs." He rubbed his thumb across his fingers. "I'm just glad she had the life she wanted."

"And you, Jim? What did you do?"

"The best I could."

There isn't much more to tell from there on. That's sad to say, I suppose that my story ended fifty years back, but it's the truth. Everything after Riot's fight and Katherine leaving was more of the same; I just got older. Riot didn't, or not outwardly, anyway. He just kept swaggering along, with his battle scars, but no limp and no cataracts, not even a loose tooth for decades. Over the years I've told people that he died and that I got a new puppy who looked just like him. I'm not sure if they believed me, but what else are they going to think? I tend not to worry about it. There've been scant few people who got close enough to disturb the lie.

Dad noticed, of course. He lived until 1992, when Riot should have been dead and buried three times over, and there was no way I was going to convince *him* that this was a different dog, who just happened to have the same markings and who was so utterly thrilled every time my old man popped round to visit.

One time he asked me about it and I just told him that Riot must have good genes. "Like me," I said.

"Oh, I don't know about that, son," he said. "I'm not to be trusted. Watch your ticker." Then he stared at Riot for a long time, until finally the dog got tired of the game and leapt into his lap.

"You've always been a strange creature," Dad said. Then I watched him push the mystery aside. "Good boy, Riot. You live forever."

We didn't see the boggart again for seventeen years. No one else was taken, or harmed, and those two kids we saved must not have told their parents anything because there was never any outcry about a monster, nor about a strange young man and his dog running amok at the Square. All was quiet, and whether it's 'cos we scared the boggart away, or because we just did our job every single day, well, it doesn't matter. We made it safe.

Complacency catches all of us out in the end.

One morning in the summer of eighty-seven, I woke up early with the idea to take Riot to the seaside. It dawned on me that he'd never been to a beach and, though I'd begun to come to terms with all the bright wide life that I was missing, it only struck me that day how Riot's life had been just as narrow. He was a good boy and he deserved to see the ocean.

We should have gone up to the Square first and got it done early, but we would've missed the bus. The coach to Morecambe had us there by lunchtime and I assumed we'd have an hour or two and be back well in time.

Remember, it had been nearly two decades since we'd seen head nor hair of the boggart; I was overconfident.

Riot ran... well, riot. He chased gulls, pounced into the tidal pools, and when we made the long walk out to the sea that never seems to come in on that beach, he met the surging water like an old friend, with all of his usual strutting self-assurance. We walked back to the pier and he sat by me on a bench, eating chips that I'd sucked free of salt. He had the kind of day that I think dogs dream about, the kind I hope they charge into forever when they die.

On the way back we hit traffic and Riot started getting anxious. First he huffed, then he howled and by the time we were moving again, he'd peed all over the floor. I remember how it pooled around this old dear's shoes. The driver went mad. If we weren't in the middle of a motorway, he'd have thrown us off.

Riot was going off like a fire alarm by the time we got back to Symester and all the way up the lane I remembered the promise I'd made, never to put him in a position where he had to face that thing again. This time, I decided, if anyone had to fight, it would be me.

Thank heavens, there were no children in the Square that afternoon, but the boggart was there, in his grey clothes, trying to fit with our world and missing by about four decades. Though he saw us arrive, he didn't approach, nor did I release Riot.

"What do you want?" I shouted.

He took a moment before replying, as if trying to work out why we neither fled nor attacked.

"We're hungry," he said, eventually.

"What do you mean *we*? It's just you."

"Many of us," he said. "All hungry."

All through this halting conversation, me and Riot walked our circuit, slowly and with great focus, never once taking our eyes of the boggart, who was sloping toward the gate.

If we'd manged to ward all four sides of the field before he left would Riot's spell have been reversed? Would we have trapped him *inside* the Square? What would have happened then, I wondered? Maybe whoever owned that field would have come forward. Maybe then we'd get to the bottom of why this town has let its horrors happen without enquiry.

It's a moot point. The boggart slipped out, but rather than vanish, he waited for us as we walked along the final edge of the field. Finally, we stood either side of the gate. I was trembling with nerves, Riot with purpose, and the boggart with a face full of hate beneath the brim of his quarryman's cap.

"I'll be here when you're gone," he said. "I abide." His words collapsed into that grating unspeech, no language a sane mind could grasp. Then he showed me his final party trick, one that could unspin the threads of my mind, if I let it. With one arm he delved into his overalls, sinking the limb all the way to his shoulder. He repeated the gesture with his other arm, then ducked his head and dove into himself, like a coat that packs down into its own pocket. In a half-moment he was gone, into whatever dark fold of the universe he called home, and there was only the wet smack of air rushing into the space he vacated.

That was thirty eight years ago and we've not seen him since. He made true on his threat in the end, of course. He outlasted Riot – the Hoyle boy is proof of that – and he'll certainly outlast me. But we did our best for as long as we could.

We maintained our vigil constantly, and this time I really did keep my promise to Riot: not once have we risked giving that horror an open window. I can count on one hand the nights I've gone to sleep outside of Symester, and yes, it's been lonely at times, and worse, boring, but it was safe. I taught for twenty-odd years at the high school and got on well with most of my colleagues. Made a few good friends, even. As for more, well, now and then I've had company for a week or a month, almost a year once with Fiona, the barmaid who saved my dad's life. She was kind and she required nothing of me but, in the end, it's always too hard a secret to keep, and the truth is too much to expect of someone else. Mostly it's just been me and Riot against the world. And I wouldn't want anyone to pity me. A lot of people go through their whole lives without ever having a single friend as good as mine.

Riot started to get old about a year ago. The first thing I noticed was a few patches of grey in his muzzle. In the firelight they shone silver, just like his crown.

For a while, I chose not to think about what that could mean. He still walked miles with me every day; he was still eating well, and if he didn't zoom around the front room as much as he used to, well ... we all grow up, don't we? But then there was a morning in the New Year, when he didn't come down for breakfast. He was always lazy on winter weekends, 'cos he'd gotten used to me staying in bed and reading for an hour or two before we both confronted the day. The clatter of his bowl always brought him down eventually, but that morning, there was no thump as he hit the bedroom floor. When I went up to fetch him, I found him standing on the edge of the bed, afraid to jump. His bad paw – the one the boggart injured – was hurting him for the first time in sixty-odd years. He looked at me with a helpless look, and there was shame in it.

"Don't worry about it, boy," I said. "We all have rough days." I carried him downstairs and by that afternoon, he'd recovered. We didn't speak about it.

Over the next few months, it was a sequence of minor problems: a temporary limp, an upset stomach, things like that. Getting up to the Square started taking a little longer each week and by summer, I was carrying him down on most days.

I knew what was happening, of course. All of his years and all of the responsibility, it was catching up with him, and all at once. In six months, he changed from a dog in the prime of life, to a tired old bear who dozed most of the day by the fire.

My mate was dying.

I wanted to stop patrolling, to let him rest. Not Riot, though. No matter how tired he was, he would still make his way to the door once the afternoon rolled around. The one time I told him, *no, that's enough, we've done enough,* he barked at me until I conceded. He was right, of course. What a waste it would've been to devote his life to one job, only to shirk it at the end.

Friday was our last shift. I didn't know, but I think he did. For the last few weeks, he'd really been struggling to walk any distance. The vet said that arthritis had colonised most of Riot's joints, and he'd begun to move with a stiff-legged hop, as if the entire back half of his body was carved from a single piece of wood. But no matter how long it took us to get round that field, I still threw his tennis ball for him a time or two as reward, and he still hobbled after it like it was the greatest treasure.

On Friday I threw the ball and Riot just sat by my feet and let it roll away. He didn't seem to be in any pain, or no more than his newly old bones were used to. And he gave no sign of being unhappy, quite the opposite: he sat calm and serene, leaning in a little against my calf. He just didn't feel like chasing the ball. He was done with that.

That ball is still out there, uncollected. That seems right.

Riot died that evening without fuss or fanfare. We had our dinner and he sat in my lap whilst I stroked his ears and he set to snoring. I was watching a game show on the telly and I don't know how long he lay there before I realised the snoring had stopped.

It was his eyes that told me the truth, a pair of rain-washed pebbles that had lost their shine.

The word heartbreak suggests a snap or a shatter, a sudden, violent before-and-after. For me, it was gentler – like my heart was water turning to steam – but, in the end, pain is pain. I pressed my face to his still-warm fur and discovered that I was a crying man after all. I cried for my mam and dad, and Katherine, and Emily Lumb and her hopeless mam, and I cried for Bobby Booth, and Herbie who was never my friend quite so much after what happened to his brother, and I cried for myself, and this long life that was always less than I wish it had been.

Mostly, I was crying 'cos I loved Riot, but Riot was gone.

Leavings

THAT FINAL WORD, *GONE*, cracked and fell like a stone into the silent well of Margie's kitchen. She kept quiet, giving Jim time to push all his exposed edges back inside himself. At last, he blinked, swallowed, and drummed his fingers on the tabletop in a busy rhythm that meant *I'm ok. Done. Move on.*

"I'm so sorry, Jim." It was the only possible thing to say.

"Thanks, Margie."

"How are you coping? When you aren't three sheets on cheap whisky and telling your life story to strangers, I mean?" They shared a chuckle at the absurdity, then Jim's face fell serious.

"For a day I took some comfort in the thought that Riot's death meant the boggart was gone, too. That they'd worn down on the same cosmic egg timer. Course, that makes no sense, even considering the mad logic of everything I've told you. All of that." He gestured to the neatly stacked pile of notes. "It says Riot is just one in a long line of good boys defending that ground." Jim's breath hitched. "I just wanted *my* good boy to be the one who won."

"But then Andy..." Margie said.

"Aye. I hung on to hope all through Saturday and Sunday, and then I heard about him going missing. Oh, it crushed me flat, Margie. I won't lie, I had a dark night that night. One of the darkest of my life." His face made it clear there would be no details forthcoming.

"But you picked yourself up."

He nodded. "I got up Monday morning, threw the bottles away, and I thought, no, this can't be it. There's no world that is cruel enough to take my life, and his life," he thumbed at the holdall and continued, "and just let us smash ourselves to bits for no gain. Like I told you out there, Margie, there was so much Riot inside that little body, I reckon at least some of it must be left over."

"What does that mean, left over?"

"I'm not sure," he admitted. "But I know that Collie dog saved George, and how he said it came from that long grass. I remember how they found a dog's body in there in the days before I first had a run in with the boggart. And then how Riot appeared – and I wondered, if I brought his body here..."

It felt like he was making a point, but Margie struggled to join it together. The whisky had really walloped her. She needed tea, though it was late and would no doubt have her up in the early hours, not that she thought she would sleep much tonight with this story ricocheting in her head. She offered to make Jim a cup, but he demurred.

"Not for me. Very kind of you to offer and to listen to me yarn on. But I have to bury my friend."

Ah, yes. She'd forgotten that unfortunate feature of the evening. Margie supposed she should dissuade him from burying a dog in the field behind her house, a place where children played. She should outright forbid it.

"Can I help you, Jim?"

"Thank you," he said. "But no. It was just me and him for his whole life. It should be just me and him for this."

Jim lifted his leg down from the foot stool. He cringed in anticipation of pain, then looked pleasantly surprised. "See, told you it sorts itself out."

He was preparing to leave.

"Wait, Jim."

Margie had thought of many questions over the last – she checked the clock – *five hours!* She'd compiled them, revised them, and refreshed them with each new piece of information. Now though, she found she only had one that required an answer.

"Am I the first person you ever told this story to?"

"Aye,"

"But you don't know me from Eve."

He looked almost amused. "Perhaps that's why, Margie. How much would it really have mattered if you think I'm mad? No offense meant."

"None taken," she said. "But, for the record, I don't think you are. Mad, I mean."

"No lass, I don't expect you do."

It had been a while since anyone had called Margie lass. She found she liked it. For the first time she considered what would happen if she invited him to stay. They'd both sunk enough whisky and lived enough years to forgo embarrassment, but she suspected neither of them really desired that sweet lie. Not after a night of such bitter truths.

"Really, Jim, why did you tell me your story?"

There was still humour in his gaze but also a weighing, an appraisal.

"I told you because I can't do what come's next."

"What comes next?"

"I don't know but something will."

Jim moved toward the door.

"I think I'm a good person, Margie. Not perfect but I did my best." He picked up the bag. "And I had help."

He opened the door and cold air flooded the room. "You're a good person, too, I think. Probably better than me. Keep an eye out, and an ear, and a hand if needed."

"For what?" she asked, an inexplicable panic bubbling in her chest.

Jim just smiled. "I'm going now, Margie. I'm going to bury my friend then go home and sleep. It's been wonderful talking to you. Thanks for the tea and the whisky. And the warmth."

He was leaving and she supposed that was fine, but she wanted to know something else.

"What will you do tomorrow?"

For a second he looked uneasy, as if he'd glanced down and seen the floor falling away beneath him. It was with evident will that he thrust his shoulders back and stood straight.

"I thought I might be free."

He closed the door politely behind him and Margie watched through the window as he made his way down her garden and back to the Square, taking his shovel from where he'd left it leaning against her fence. The clouds had moved on and the moon was full enough for Margie to watch him complete the small grave. She watched him hoist the holdall to his chest and embrace it, before placing it reverently where it could rest. He filled the hole in quickly and only when it was done did he kneel down – *oh, how his back must ache* – and place a hand – *his marked hand* – against the ground. She didn't know what words he said, but she suspected he was speaking of love and loyalty and a job well done.

On his way to the gate, he stopped and bent down once more. He picked something up from the ground and Margie wasn't sure – as he was a mere silhouette now – but she thought he was laughing. He tossed it in the air and caught it with the same hand.

A small object, about the size of a tennis ball.

In a smooth, practiced movement, he launched the ball across the Square. Margie tried to track it, but it flew high and invisible into the night. When she turned back, he was at the gate, then through it, then away.

Four weeks later, she woke to the pebbling of hail against her bedroom window. November had arrived, vicious and indifferent to the bones of ageing women, and Margie lay in her pocket of warmth, thinking today could be the day she cast off habit and stayed in bed. Duty proved stronger than indulgence, however, and by quarter past seven she was in the kitchen, waiting for her tea to brew and watching the first chrome streak of morning rise above the Square.

As it had so many times in recent days, her mind turned to Andy Hoyle, who the police were no closer to finding, and whose mother's tortured pleas for information were now beginning to slip from the nightly bulletins. They were never going to find him, Margie knew. He had gone somewhere the police could not search, and all she could wish for him now was peace.

From that tragedy, her thoughts spun on, as they always did, to Jim Howarth. For two days after his visit, Margie had stayed in her house, deliberating over what to do. Should she go to the police and report a mentally ill man, who told stories about monsters and guardian mongrels? Or should she let him go pursue whatever freedom he so richly deserved, if his story was true.

Don, unsurprisingly, had firm opinions on the matter.

You have to tell someone, Margie. He could be dangerous.

I believed him.

Yes, but you'd had a lot to drink. And you felt sorry for him.

But all that documentation?

Surely you can see he found that first, and built his story around it?

That photo of Riot in '69!

A different dog that just looked similar.

Finally, she took the middle road between Don's pragmatism and her own quiet yearning for the peculiar. She drove down to the village, with no clear plan in mind, but a need to close the wound Jim's story had torn in her worldview. If she could find him and ask him some questions in the stark light of day, she knew she'd be able to dispel whatever candlelit magic he'd woven around her in her kitchen.

Sifting through his story for a place to begin, she made her way to the Bell and Kettle. It was a tawdry looking pub on Bridge Street, missing letters from its sign and shingles from its roof. A bored looking barman listened to her description of Jim, told her to wait one minute and then ducked into the back. When he emerged, he was accompanied by a woman around Margie's own age, wearing rust coloured overalls and a short chop of hair dyed a bright cartoonish pink.

"You after Jim Howarth?" she asked, with more than a little suspicion.

"Yes, do you know him?" Margie asked.

"Only for the last fifty years. We go back, me and Jim. I'm Fiona Haltwhistle, the landlady. Do you mind me asking who you are?"

"Margie Jones. I met Jim the other night and I'd like to talk to him again."

Fiona's face lit up. "Ah, so you're Margie. We've been taking bets on whether you'd be in!"

"I'm sorry?" Margie said, startled.

"Jim left something for you before he went?"

"Went, went where?"

"God knows. He came in the night before last, as we're shutting up, and he tells me you'll be in asking for him, and to give you this."

Fiona rummaged under the bar and handed Margie an envelope. It was creased and stained with a beer ring, but her name was written on the front in neat, serrated handwriting.

"He said he was off and asked me to look after his house. Barmy if you ask me, suddenly going off galivanting, after all these years of not going more than three miles from his front door. But Jim always was a strange one. Lovely bloke, we had some good times together, but he was a man of habits, you know, like a lot of bachelors."

Fiona seemed to realise how much she was divulging to a stranger.

"Anyway," she said, "losing his dog might have finally given him the push he needed. He had that dog a long time. A long, long time." Was there a flicker in Fiona's face? An awareness of things best left unpursued? "Did you meet the dog?"

"Riot?" Margie said. "Oh yes, he was a brave little thing."

"Yeah, he was."

Margie felt like she'd passed a test.

"Sorry you missed Jim but hopefully that'll explain it." Fiona pointed to the envelope, eyes hungry for answers. "Can I get you a drink?"

"Oh, no. Must get back." Margie said her thanks and left the pub in a hurry.

Back in the car she tore open the envelope and extracted the brief note that was folded inside. Before she could read it, two small objects slipped out of the crease and landed in her palm. A pair of small tin discs with fixing loops attached. One was blank and unblemished. Pressed into the other, edges dulled by age, were four bold letters.

RIOT

She swallowed down a sudden choke of emotion and opened the note. It was very brief, but Margie looked at it for a long time.

Dear Margie,

These may come in handy. Or they may not. But, if you cared enough to try to find me, you are the right person to leave them with.

Be well. Do not repent of your life.

Sincerely,

James Howarth

A month later, the note was still pinned to her fridge. She read it daily, trying to tease out any deeper meaning to be found in Jim's advice. There was no repentance of her life, of that she was confident, having thought on it often in the last few weeks. She'd loved Don firmly and faithfully for all of their marriage. There hadn't been children, but there hadn't ever been a true want for them. Don had been enough, in all of his fustiness and restraint, just as Symester had been enough of a home these last forty years. Not a glamorous life but she didn't feel cheated, or in need of Jim's lesson.

"Patronising bugger," she said aloud.

That said, she had to admit that there had perhaps been too many lonely moments in recent years. In her grief and her impatience, she'd swept her life clean of strife but, in doing so, had she cleaned up too much of the mess that makes a life something more than just being awake? Sometimes, she thought, the dissatisfaction of stillness only became clear in the act of disturbance. Throw a stone into calm water and the ripples are their own kind of beauty.

Margie's ripple arrived one week after Jim's visit, a few days following her trip to the Bell and Kettle, when she was still in an agony of indecision over what to do. It arrived as a scratch at the door in the middle of the night, a puling wail that made Margie question her belief in spirits. After what Jim had told her about the land outside her house, she was newly spooked by a whole range of ideas that she would once have mocked. She still watched the apple tree from her kitchen, but now she cast her attention wider, watching for a stray figure, a flash of grey.

She'd tiptoed to her front door and peered through the glass panel to check there was no hulking murderer on the other side. Whilst Don had a merry old tantrum in her head, Margie fetched her keys and unlocked the door. The crying was too much, and she was half convinced that some young girl in a bad way had left her baby to be discovered. The other half of her was already convinced of what awaited.

With an open door, the noise got immediately louder. It was coming from the bottom of her garden and, paying no mind to the blanket of drizzle that sucked her nightdress to her skin, Margie made her way barefoot down the path. Six feet from the gate she halted.

Do I really want this, she thought?

Can I do this?

Just go back to bed, love. Don spoke in the calm tones he always used to dissuade her from her more outlandish notions. *You don't need this trouble. Go to bed and let it be someone else's problem.*

Be quiet, Don, she thought, gently. I love you but shush now.

She opened the gate and looked down at the small shape lying and crying in the mucky overspill of the Square.

"Hello, trouble," she said.

That was three weeks ago. Now, as the hail softened to a pounding rain that still rattled the windows, Margie took a sip of hot tea and shuffled to the crate in the corner of the kitchen. The creature inside was a bundle of black and tan fur and oversize limbs. Baby German Shepherds always looked like that, she'd read, half-wolf, half-sock puppet. But the eyes. Margie thought the eyes were the purest things she'd ever seen.

She unclasped the crate and the puppy tumbled out, already leaping up at Margie in excitement.

"Good boy," she said, tousling the spot between his ears, that white spot that she'd stared at with such doubt and anxiety in the first few days.

The dog bounded to the front door and barked once, expectantly.

Margie glanced at the window where rain distorted the Square into a murky green mirage. She laughed. "Not yet, Trouble. Let's have a cuddle and some breakfast, and we'll make our rounds when it brightens up."

The dog cocked his head in puzzlement and barked once more, a note of anxiety edging in.

"Hey, don't start that. I'm in charge" Margie asserted, then sweetened her tone. "Don't worry, boy. I won't forget."

As if understanding her promise, Trouble crossed the room to her, the tin name tag hanging from his collar tinkling as he moved. He came to rest by her feet, tail thumping against the floor, and he stared up at her through bright pebble eyes, just happy to be alive.

Acknowledgements

Thanks are in order. So many that, were it to give full vent, I'd double the length of this book. So, to keep things brief:

First, to Ariell Cacciola, who invited me to be part of this splendid project. A more generous, cheerful and patient editor you could not find. Welcome to the North!

To Claire Holliday, who kept me sane with kindness during the sprint to finish.

To Rachel Harrison, who read it before anyone else and gave me a high-ball injection of confidence when it was most sorely needed. Cheers, Buddy!

To Nat Cassidy, Ka-brother, who feels the beating heart of a story (and a Springsteen lyric) better than anyone else I know. Your meandering voice notes are a constant, if time-consuming joy.

Gemma Amor is just about the savviest and most loyal friend it's possible to have in this business of scary stories. Cheers for all the advice, the nudges in the right direction, and the cautionary tales when necessary. You're ace!

And thanks to Stephen King for … well … everything. You've been told so many times what you mean to us, so I won't bore you with repetition. But it's privilege to have met you, and a mad dream to have sent you my story.

Cheers to the Dross lads who have shouted me on in creative life, just as loudly as they do when we're racing. Love to Stu, Chris, D, and Baines who will find things to mock in this earnest little tale, but who will buy it anyway. 'Cos that's what mates do.

Thanks to Stefi, Steve, Tom and Bhavi – for all the love, acceptance, cheerleading and lasagne. Better in-laws do not exist.

To Giorgia, who shouldn't need a message in a book to know what she means to me, 'cos I should show her every single day. Twice the wins, love! The snort was always based on you.

To my mum, who quietly gets on with the business of keeping me afloat, expecting nothing, giving everything. Lots of love mam; you are quite literally, the best.

And to my dad, who went and bloody died with the worst possible timing before he ever got to hold my book in his hands. But he read it, and loved it, and that will do for me.

About the Author

Neil McRobert is a writer, podcaster and recovering academic. He fled the haunted halls of higher education to settle in an old Northern village, where he writes about scary things and runs the landmark horror podcast, *Talking Scared*. When he's not reading, writing or interviewing famous horror novelists, he's out in the fields with his dog, Ted.

Instagram @talkscaredpod
Twitter @TalkScaredPod
Bluesky @talkscaredpod.bsky.social

About The Northern Weird Project

This book is a part of The Northern Weird Project by Wild Hunt Books, a collection of six pocket-sized novellas by authors who are writing and living in the North of England.

Incorporating eerie and uncanny incidents, these novellas investigate aspects of the North through setting, subject and character.

All books in this series are available to order from our bookshop.
https://www.wildhuntbooks.co.uk/bookshop

More From The Northern Weird Project

This House Isn't Haunted But We Are
by Stephen Howard

Simon and Priya's young daughter has died in a tragic accident. Determined to heal their fracturing marriage, the couple move to the North Yorkshire Moors to renovate a dilapidated rural cottage. However, they just can't process their grief as increasingly eerie events unfold. A child's ghostly figure appears on the moors, doors lock themselves, and a mysterious stain grows from the loft. Is it their daughter haunting them or something else?

(Don't) Call Mum
by Matt Wesolowski

Leo is just trying to catch his train back home to the village of Malacstone in North East England. But there's disorder at the station, and when a loud young man heading for London boards the train accidentally, a usually easy journey descends into darkness and chaos. The train soon breaks down in the middle of nowhere, and as night falls, something...or someone steps out of the distance. Is it a man or something far more sinister?

The Off-Season
by Jodie Robins

It's the off-season in the seaside resort town of Blackpool, where Tommy never imagined he would return. His relationship has broken down, so he returns home to keep an eye on his widowed father. While counting down the hours before attending the funeral of a well-loved friend, a mysterious group turns up on the seafront. One by one, the locals are entranced by their presence until Tommy and his father can no longer resist the allure. Tommy soon discovers a secret desire his father has been harbouring for his entire life.

The Retreat
by Gemma Fairclough

Richard's sister Julie returns home from a mysterious wellness facility in remote Cumbria in 1994. He's convinced that this place was a cult and was the cause of his sister's eventual suicide. Finally, after years as an unaccomplished academic, he decides to investigate the disturbing accusations against the Hartman Retreat Centre. Then he meets Lucy, a young woman whose story is eerily similar to his sister's decades before. Richard is determined to unearth what's really been happening at the Hartman Retreat Centre but more importantly, who is Charles Hartman, the celebrated healer who casts a powerful hold over all who come to the retreat.

Turbine 34
by Katherine Clements

It's 2035 and England is experiencing the hottest summer in living memory. A 61-year-old environmental scientist is tasked with evaluating the impact of a controversial new wind farm on the West Yorkshire moors. Camped out alone at Turbine 34 which was built on the ancient peat bog, she soon discovers signs of the devastation caused by the construction, she begins to see things that shouldn't be there. She has dedicated her life to protecting the moor, but will it protect her?

Wild Hunt Books would like to thank the following Lifetime Supporters:

Daniel Sorabji
Jan Penovich
Blaise Cacciola

BECOME A SUPPORTER BY CONTACTING US AT
INFO@WILDHUNTBOOKS.CO.UK

The Publisher would also like to thank the following early supporters of The Northern Weird Project:

Aidan Smith
Alex Herod
Ali W
Alicia Lomas-Gross
Anthony Martin
Beth Baskett
Bethany Vare
Blair Rose
Carmen
Charlotte Platt
Charlotte Tierney
Emma Armshaw
Freya S
George Dunn
Heidi Marjamäki
Ianthe May
J. Aaron Courts CWO4, USMC, Retired
Jeff
Jennifer B. Lyday
K. Wicks
Kelsey Stoddard
Kirsty Logan
Laura Elliott
Lisa Elliott
Lynne G
Mandy Bublitz
Mark Taylor

Martyn Waites
Monica Voynovska
Nicola Leedham
Nina Woodcock
Rachel Bridgeman
Rosie Warfield
Samuel Best
Sheena E. Perez
Sonja Zimmermann
Sophy Holland
Stefanie Olivola
Stephanie Eleanor Henrichs Welch
Stewart Mack
Vince Fairclough